Kiss Me Forever

BACHELORS & BRIDESMAIDS (#1)

BARBARA FREETHY

Coming Soon
In the Bachelors and Bridesmaids series

Steal My Heart *(#2)*
All Your Loving *(#3)*

Chapter One

"You're done, Andrea," Roger Thornton said.

The editor-in-chief of *World News Today* had always been blunt, but his statement seemed a little harsh even for him. Andrea Blain sat up straighter as she faced her boss across the massive desk in his office. "Done as in fired?" she asked warily.

"You're not fired, but you're close. Do you know how much money we've spent the last six weeks helping you chase a story that turned out to be nothing?"

"It's not nothing. I just need more time to gather evidence."

"You don't need time. You need to refocus. You had a hunch; it didn't pay off."

"My source got scared off. I'll find someone else."

"It took you weeks to find him. Cut your losses."

She could not believe Roger was going to pull her off the story she'd been working on the past two months. She'd been talking to a potential whistleblower at a company that made car seats for children. There had been two fatal accidents involving the car seats in the last year. "If my hunch is right, my story could save lives."

"You'll have to work on it on your own time. If you had some real evidence, maybe I could give you another week, but all you have is a disgruntled employee and a lawsuit that was thrown out of court for lack of evidence."

"I also have two injured children," she reminded him.

"There's no concrete evidence the car seats were to blame."

"Not yet. But I think I can get it."

He frowned. "I'm sorry Andrea. You're out of time. I can't carry reporters on my staff who aren't actually reporting."

"Some stories take time to develop," she argued. "You know that."

Roger took off his glasses and rubbed a hand across his weary eyes. He was a big bear of a man, well over six feet tall and at least two hundred and fifty pounds. At age fifty-six, he'd been in the news business longer than she'd been alive, and she had a great deal of respect for him.

"I do know that, Andrea, and ten years ago I would have let you have that time. But we now operate on a 24-hour news cycle. If we don't have new content, we don't have readers. More importantly we don't have advertisers. We're struggling to stay alive in a world where most people get their news off of social media. I can't have reporters working on stories for weeks at a time. It's not cost effective."

"I understand the challenges—" she began.

He quickly cut her off. "It doesn't matter what you understand. We're moving on. I have a new story for you, one that will give you an opportunity to show the owners of this magazine that you actually work here, and that they have a reason to pay you a salary."

"What's the story?" she asked with a sigh, knowing that if the orders came from the top floor, there was no point in arguing any further.

Roger picked up a manila folder and pushed it across the desk to her. "Alexander Donovan."

"Who?" she asked, not sure she had heard him correctly.

"You know who he is. Alexander Donovan will be the magazine's *Man of the Year*, and you're going to write the cover story."

"Alexander Donovan is going to be our *Man of the Year?*" she echoed in disbelief. "Why? He makes computer games. He's a rich playboy. We should have someone serious on the cover, someone who is making a difference in the world. This is not my style." Andrea tossed the folder down on the desk and got to her feet.

Restlessness propelled her to the window. Ten floors below lay the busy streets of San Francisco, the city where she had come to find her dreams. *World News Today* was one of the top news magazines in the country, focusing on serious issues, politics, foreign policy and the global economy. The cover story was usually a plum job, one she would have loved to have if it had been anyone else, but Roger's choice of *Man of the Year* made the assignment seem like a joke. She turned back to face him. "Why are you doing this? Is the magazine changing focus?"

"Not at all. Alexander Donovan does more than make games. He's a philanthropist. He donates millions of dollars to schools and charity organizations. He runs camps for underprivileged children. He sends medical supplies to Africa. In a time when the world has become increasingly cynical, Alexander Donovan is the embodiment of generosity and hope."

"In other words, he's a master of public relations," she said cynically.

"He is a master, but don't close your eyes to the possibilities. I know this isn't your style. To be frank, it's not mine, either, but our publisher is convinced that Donovan will sell a lot more copies than some over-photographed politician. The cover will bring in readers that don't normally pick up the magazine. Your job is to keep them reading."

"How on earth will I do that?"

"Do what you do well, Andrea—find an angle."

"And if I can't?"

"Then you may want to start looking for another job."

She blew out a quick breath at his blunt statement. "It's that serious?"

"It is."

"So Alexander Donovan is my get-out-of-the-doghouse card?"

"Exactly."

Andrea sat back down in her chair and picked up Donovan's folder. "I don't know what you think I'm going to find that no one else has. I'm sure he's been interviewed dozens of times."

"He's been photographed thousands of times, but he hasn't done any in-depth interviews outside the celebrity magazine circuit. All we know about him is that he was born in Los Angeles. His parents died in an automobile accident when he was twelve. He went to live with his aunt. She died when he was seventeen. After that he made it on his own, no other relatives, not too many close friends. He made his first million before he was twenty-five years old, without the benefit of a college degree, and he hasn't looked back since. That was seven years ago. At thirty-two he is ranked among the top thirty wealthiest men in the country."

"That's amazing," she admitted.

"He's a success story, and people like to read about success stories, especially rags to riches. Our readership is primarily male, but Alexander Donovan will bring in the women. He's young, attractive and a billionaire."

"What more could a woman want?" she asked dryly.

"Exactly. But I want more from you than a fluff piece. I may have been pushed to put this man on the cover, but you're going to find me some reasons why he belongs there."

"All right. I'll do Alex Donovan." She stopped abruptly, realizing what she'd just said. "I mean, I'll interview him," she added hastily, ignoring Roger's grin.

"He's expecting you at his office in one hour."

"What if I have other plans? It's Friday night. I could have a date."

He raised an eyebrow. "You haven't had a date in months."

"Well, it's not because I haven't been asked," she grumbled.

"Oh, I know that, Andrea. You're a beautiful woman, but you're a workaholic, and while I appreciate your dedication, I know from firsthand experience that all work and no play equals burnout."

"Then why did you schedule a job for me on a Friday night?" she challenged.

"That was at Donovan's request. He's going to let you shadow him this weekend. I want to put this story to bed by the first of October. That gives you ten days. And one last thing—Donovan is not a stupid man. He also has a great deal of money and power. You're going to triple check every fact in your article. The last thing I need is a lawsuit."

The last thing she needed as well. "Got it."

She walked out of Roger's office and down the hall to her cubicle. It was in the far end of the newsroom and boasted one small window that overlooked downtown San Francisco. If she stood on her tiptoes at a certain angle, she could actually see the Golden Gate Bridge. Not that she ever took much time to look at the view—she was usually buried in her work. She loved her job, and she wanted to keep it. While she'd agreed to do the Donovan article, she was going to continue to work on her other story on the side.

Sitting down behind her desk, she opened the file of clippings Roger had given her. The photo on top was a picture of a man and woman leaving a party. The man was dressed in a sleek black tuxedo. He was tall with dark hair, a square face and a strong jaw. He was caught in midstride, the power of his movement clear even through the fuzziness of the photo. The expression on his face was a mixture of amusement and annoyance, and there was something about the thrust of his chin that seemed downright challenging.

The woman was pure eye candy, long cascading blonde hair, big breasts spilling out of a very tight and short dress.

Andrea sighed, turning the photo several different ways as she studied her next assignment. Did Alexander Donovan's eyes hide some sort of a mystery? Or was he just a good-looking man with too much money and too many women?

Whatever he was, she could handle it. She could handle anyone, as long as he wasn't a complete bore. Dull and uninteresting would mean death to her career—a career that was apparently on thin ice.

Her cell phone buzzed and she picked it up, seeing her friend Kate's number flash across the screen. "Hey, what's up?"

"I can't believe you actually answered your phone," Kate said. "You've been missing in action the last few weeks."

"Work," she said, knowing her friends were getting tired of that excuse, but it was the truth. She'd been so obsessed with her last investigation into the car seat manufacturer that she'd put everything else in her life on hold. She just wished she had something to show for all that time.

"We all work, Andrea," Kate reminded her. "But I didn't call you up to give you a lecture. Laurel and I are grabbing drinks tonight to discuss her bachelorette party. She said she's texted you several times but you haven't answered."

A wave of guilt ran through her. Her twin sister Laurel was getting married in a few weeks, and she wasn't doing a great job as the maid of honor. "I can't do drinks tonight. I have a work assignment. But I will try to be at brunch on Sunday. We can talk then."

"What kind of work do you have on a Friday night?"

"I've been assigned the cover story on Alexander Donovan, and he's agreed to let me shadow him this weekend."

"What?" Kate asked with a surprised squeal. "Are you serious? Are you telling me that you're going out tonight with *Celeb Magazine's 'Sexiest Man Alive'?*"

Andrea quickly leafed through the clippings in the folder in front of her, landing on the cover Kate had just mentioned. "I didn't realize," she said, a little mesmerized by the shot of a bare-chested Alexander Donovan. The man obviously did more than sit behind a desk all day. His abs were ripped.

"Where are you going with him?" Kate asked.

"I don't know yet. I have to meet him at his office in an hour."

"This is so exciting. He's attractive, single and rich. The two of you could fall in love."

Andrea laughed. Kate was a wedding planner and had been a romantic for as long as Andrea had known her. "You're crazy. This is just a job. And I'm sure the man has a girlfriend, probably more than one."

"Well, you never know. I can't wait to hear how it goes. Call me tonight. Or if it's too late, first thing in the morning, and don't forget brunch on Sunday. If you're not there, I will come and find you."

"I honestly can't promise I'll be there. It depends on where this story goes."

"Fine. If you're in bed with Alexander Donovan, you get a pass. Otherwise, you better be there."

She rolled her eyes. "I'm not dating him; I'm interviewing him."

"We'll see."

"You have love on the brain."

Kate laughed. "I do. How can I help it? I'm surrounded every day with joyous brides. I want us all to have that same feeling one day."

"Well, Laurel has it," Andrea said, thinking of how happy her sister was to be in love and engaged. She couldn't even imagine getting to that point. Right now, a great date would be a welcome surprise. Her track record with men the last few years was not impressive. "I'll talk to you later. I have to get ready."

"Wear something sexy."

"Goodbye, Kate," she said with laugh. As she set down her phone, she picked up the photo of Alexander Donovan again. His sexy, laughing gaze made butterflies dance through her stomach. "Just an assignment," she told herself again. A story she needed to do well if she wanted to keep her job.

* * *

"You cannot escape the Raven's deadly shot." Alexander Donovan said the words with greedy intensity as he skillfully outmaneuvered the approaching monstrous villain known as Gaya.

"Gaya can outjump Raven." Thirteen-year-old Tyler Parker sent his warrior jumping into space with a quick maneuver.

"Not bad, but you made one mistake."

Tyler groaned as Alex's character turned the carpet into a missile that destroyed Gaya into a shattering kaleidoscope of color. "That's not fair."

"It's fair. I introduced the missile two levels ago," Alex said, sitting back in his chair as he watched the game calculate his award points on the sixty-inch flat screen television that hung on the wall of his office.

While he made video games and apps, he still loved computer games the best. He could add so many more complications, so many more opportunities to change plays with a variety of keystrokes. He pushed the keyboard away and smiled at the frustrated kid next to him. Tyler's competitive spirit would reemerge within seconds. He just needed a second to regroup.

As he studied Tyler's face, he realized that the boy was starting to change into a man. He'd grown two inches in the last month and he now seemed all arms and legs, with teeth a little too big for his face. Soon his voice would change, and he'd grow into his size eleven shoes. With those changes would probably come more attitude, but Alex could handle it. He'd never forgotten how hard the teen years could be, especially for a kid like Tyler, a kid who was growing up in the same harsh system Alex had lived through—foster care.

He'd met Tyler two years earlier when he'd volunteered to be a Big Brother. At the time, Tyler had been living with his mother, but she'd died of cancer a year later and with no other relatives available to take care of him, Tyler had gone into the system.

"Let's play again," Tyler said.

"Sorry, I can't," he said, checking his watch. "I have a meeting in a few minutes."

"On Friday night? Shouldn't you have a date or something?"

He grinned. "As a matter of fact, I do have a date. So you need to go home."

Tyler let out a heavy sigh. "I guess."

Alex frowned. "Is everything okay with the Monroes? Are they treating you right?"

Tyler shrugged his shoulders as he stood up and dug his hands into the pockets of his jeans. "They make me go to church on Sunday."

"It's good to be exposed to religion."

"And they want to see my report cards," Tyler said with another heavy sigh.

"Imagine that."

"I'll be happy when I'm done with school," Tyler added.

"School is important."

"You didn't go to college."

"No, but I wish I'd had the chance," he said, getting to his feet. "I told you that if you make it through four years of college, you have a job waiting for you here."

"That's in a million years," Tyler said with a roll of his eyes.

Alex laughed. "Time goes faster when you get older."

"Do you want me to come by tomorrow and help you with more game research?"

"On Saturday? Don't you have something better to do?"

"The Monroes are going to visit some old lady. They don't need me around."

Alex sat down behind his desk and sent Tyler a thoughtful look, worried by the undercurrents in his tone. "Did they tell you that?"

"No, but it's not like I'm their real kid." He kicked at a spot on the carpet. "It's okay. I don't really care. They're better than some of the people I've lived with."

Alex nodded in agreement, wishing he could tell Tyler that everything would be fine. But would it? He knew firsthand how tough life could be, especially for a kid on his own. "I've got some things to do this weekend. Why don't you come by Monday after school? I'm going to test a new game that's still in early development. I could use your opinion." He liked to involve Tyler in the games for two reasons: one, to keep the kid engaged in life, and, two, because teenage boys were his target demographic.

Tyler's face lit up. "Awesome. Can I run the train once

before I go?"

Alex smiled. In addition to his game business, his company constructed some of the most sophisticated model trains in the world, and one of those trains wound its way around his office on sleek silver tracks.

Alex pushed the controller over to Tyler. "Go ahead."

While Tyler started the train, Alex checked his calendar to see what he had scheduled for the weekend: dinner tonight, sailing on the bay tomorrow and another party tomorrow night. It should be enough to keep a reporter from *World News Today* happy. He could show her the wonderful, exciting life he led. She would be dazzled, and he would be *Man of the Year*.

His smile turned into a sigh. Press was a necessary evil, but he didn't enjoy interviews, especially in-depth profiles. Hopefully, he would not have to answer too many questions.

Out of the corner of his eye, he watched the train begin its path around the office, through the tunnel, under the chair, and over the file cabinet. He'd always loved trains. And while they were only a small part of his business, they were probably his favorite part.

Tyler looked over at him in delight, his smile turning mischievous as they heard his assistant's voice outside the door. Alex gave a negative shake of his head, but as Ellen pushed the door open, Tyler hit the whistle. The shrill noise caused Ellen to take an abrupt step backward.

Tyler laughed, and Alex bit back a smile.

Ellen was a fifty-eight-year-old woman who'd been with him for the last five years, and while she was usually a good sport, she'd never been a big fan of all the games in his office.

"Very funny," Ellen said dryly. "Do I need to remind both of you that this is a place of business?"

"I better go," Tyler said quickly.

"Good idea," Alex said. "And get your homework done

before Sunday night. I don't want to have the Monroes on my case about letting you hang around here."

"I will," Tyler promised, bolting out the door.

As Tyler left, Ellen handed him an envelope. "Baseball tickets for the Cougars game next Friday night, courtesy of superstar Matt Kingsley."

"Nice," he said with a smile. "If the reporter is still around then, that will give me something else to take her to."

"Having this woman around for a week is going to be a lot different than granting a one-hour interview. I don't understand why you agreed to it," Ellen said, bewilderment in her eyes.

"They caught me in a weak moment," he admitted. "And a cover story with a lot of free press just before the launch of my next game was impossible to resist."

"She's going to be digging into your life, Alex."

"She's not going to find out anything about me that I don't want her to find out. I'm an expert at this. Trust me.

"I did some research on Andrea Blain. She covers politics and wars. She's not going to be a pushover. She's a serious journalist."

"How serious could she be if she got this story?" He stood up. "I'm not worried. I can handle her. If she starts digging in too deep, I'll just turn her in the other direction."

"That would be easy if she were a dog on a leash, but I don't think she is," Ellen replied.

"You never know. Neither of us has actually seen this woman. If she's as hard as nails, she probably has a face like my aunt's old bulldog, a big pudgy nose and a fat pink tongue. In fact..." He stopped abruptly, realizing that he and Ellen were no longer alone. A slender, blonde woman stood in the doorway, her snapping blue eyes filled with outrage.

"Please go on," she said.

"Who are you?" he asked, even though he already knew.

She gave him a grim smile. "I'm the bulldog."

Chapter Two

"Andrea Blain." Alex repeated her name while his gaze traveled slowly over her face. She did not resemble a bulldog in any way. Dressed in black pants with a short gray jacket over a silky top, she was slender and more than a little attractive. Her hair was pulled back from her face in a knot, setting off beautiful features, wide-set blue eyes, dark lashes, and a very pretty mouth that would have been even prettier if her lips weren't drawn in a tight angry line. She wasn't more than five feet and a couple of inches even with heels on, but her shoulders were stiff, and her slim body was poised in a way that exuded challenge.

He exchanged a quick look with Ellen, whose gaze said *I told you so.*

Then he stepped forward and extended his hand. "I'm Alex Donovan."

"Of course you are," Andrea replied, giving his hand a brief shake. "I already know your name. It's everything else I'm here to find out."

"This is my assistant, Ellen Hill."

Andrea nodded in the older woman's direction. "It's nice to meet you. I hope we'll have time to talk, if not today, then another time. I'm sure you must have a different perspective on our *Man of the Year*."

"He's a good employer. That's all I have to say." Ellen turned to Alex. "Do you need anything else tonight?"

"Yes," he said quickly. "I'll walk you out." He turned to the reporter. "Miss Blain, if you'd like to have a seat, I'll be right with you."

"All right," she said.

He walked Ellen into the outer office, shutting his door behind him. "Maybe you could call me in a half hour. I might need an emergency exit."

Ellen smiled as she took her purse out of a drawer. "That won't help. You've agreed to let her follow you around all weekend."

"So maybe I'll have an emergency out of town."

"I thought you weren't afraid of her."

"That was before I saw her."

"Good point. I think you should be worried."

"Because she's that good of a reporter?"

"No, because she's *that* pretty, and just your type."

"I can get a blonde any night of the week." He wasn't being arrogant; he was speaking the truth.

"But you can't get *that kind of blonde* any night of the week," she said with a sparkle in her eyes. "You've always liked a challenge, Alex. Have a good weekend. And good luck!"

He had a feeling he was going to need it.

* * *

Andrea wandered around Alex's office, unwilling to admit that her first sight of Alex Donovan had been more unsettling than she'd expected, and it wasn't just because she'd overheard him call her a bulldog; she'd been called far worse on the job. It was because he was much better looking in person than he was in the pictures she'd reviewed. His hair was a darker, richer brown, with thick waves just made for a woman's fingers to run through, and his eyes were a piercing green. His smile was also incredibly charming and sexy, which probably got him everything he wanted. He wouldn't have trouble getting women if he didn't have a penny in his pocket.

She cleared her throat, silently telling herself not to get carried away. He was just a man, after all. Actually, he might be more boy than man, she thought, noting the railroad tracks that traveled around the room, the videogames and monitors set up along one wall, the basketball hoop in the corner and the shelves of comic books. She probably shouldn't be surprised. Alex Donovan had made millions in the gaming industry. He had to have a good head for figuring out what kids wanted to play.

"Sorry for the delay," he said as he returned to the office.

She turned around to face him. "No problem. Are you ready to begin our interview?"

"I'm always ready."

"Good. I think we should set some ground rules before we begin."

Alex raised his eyebrows quizzically. "Like what?"

"As to how we'll proceed. Since we're going to be spending some time together, we should decide just how we're going to fill it. For instance—"

"I have decided." Alex cut her off in midsentence. "You're free to follow along on my activities, but they will be activities that I choose, not you. I'm only consenting to do this interview because I happen to enjoy reading your magazine."

"You read *World News Today*?" she asked doubtfully.

He met her gaze. "Does that surprise you?"

"A little," she admitted.

"So, you've already made a judgment—I thought you were here to get to know me."

"I am, and you're right."

A gleam came into his eyes. "A woman who can admit she is wrong—now I'm surprised."

"And you're also making a generalization."

He nodded. "Good point. So we table the snap judgments and generalizations?"

"All right."

"Getting back to the rules governing our interview. You may ask any question that you like, and I, in turn, will answer any question that I like."

He delivered his terms with a charming smile, but Andrea wasn't at all fooled. He was not going to make getting his story easy, at least not the story she wanted—the one that would flesh out his true character. But she wasn't going to argue the point now. She would bide her time and wait for her opportunity. Hopefully, it would come sooner rather than later. Roger had given her ten days, and she could not come up short again, not after the last six weeks.

"Well?" Alex prodded.

"Whatever you say. I certainly want you to be comfortable."

What she really wanted was to shake him up and get him to confess all sorts of scandalous secrets to her. But so far, she seemed to be the one feeling a little off balance.

"Thank you," he said. "By the way, if I offended you with the bulldog remark, I apologize. I had no idea you were standing there."

"So you're not sorry that you said it, only sorry that I heard you." She sent him a direct look and waited for him to squirm, but he didn't, and it was rather disconcerting. Instead of anger, she saw another smile play across his lips.

"Would it surprise you to know that I was very fond of my aunt's bulldog?"

His smile grew broader and more persuasive, and Andrea had to fight with herself not to respond. She decided to change the subject. "What plans do you have for this evening, Mr. Donovan? My boss mentioned something about dinner."

"Why don't you call me Alex, and I'll call you Andrea? As for tonight, I have reservations for dinner at the Crystal Terrace."

It was just what she had expected, the most expensive and trendiest restaurant in San Francisco. "Very nice. But you don't have to impress me. I'm much more interested in the real man than the image."

"Really?" he asked dryly. "Then you're the first in a long time. Let me sign one contract, and we'll go."

Andrea nodded. While he was reading through some paperwork on his desk, she walked across the room to take a closer look at the train. It was incredibly detailed she thought. Whoever had built this had done it with a great deal of love and passion.

"You can start the train if you like," Alex said.

"Oh. No, thanks."

"You can't break it. It's built for kids."

"It seems expensive."

"It is, but it's also meant to be played with. Did you ever play with trains when you were a child?"

She shook her head. "Never. I grew up with a sister and mother who both thought the only toys appropriate for girls were dolls and play kitchens."

"Then you've missed out."

She shrugged. "I wouldn't say that." Although she had wished for more variety when she was younger. She'd been a tomboy at heart.

Alex walked around his desk and flipped the switch, sending the train on its way. "My favorite story growing up was *The Little Engine That Could*. I see my life like that train, just chugging away toward the top of the mountain."

She raised an eyebrow. "Seriously? Your career is more

like the flight of a jet airplane than a slow-moving train. You made your first million before age twenty-five and seven years later you're the *Man of the Year* for *World News Today.* If that's not moving fast, I don't know what is."

Alex grinned. "You might have a point. What about you? Are you on a fast jet or a slow train?"

"Me? At the moment, I'm on a horse going backward."

Alex burst out laughing, a genuine smile crossing his lips. "You're very candid, aren't you?"

"Yes. It sometimes gets me into trouble."

"I'll bet."

"I hope you'll be just as honest with me. I want to do an in-depth story on you, Alex. I want the world to know the real you—what makes you tick, what you think about, worry about, what your vision is for the future."

"Your readers don't care about that. They just want to know who I'm dating."

"Well, I want more."

"Why did they give you this assignment?" he asked, a curious note in his voice. "I've read some of your work. It's serious and rather intense."

She was shocked that he'd read her articles and a little skeptical. "Which one did you like the most?" she challenged.

He gazed back at her. "Probably the one on pesticides in drinking water. It gave me chills. I haven't been able to turn on a faucet without thinking about it."

"That was one of my best articles," she admitted.

"So how did you get me?"

"I got lucky," she said lightly. "And I always put one hundred percent into my work, no matter what the assignment."

"Will this cover story help you get that horse you're on turned in the right direction?"

He was definitely a smart man, she thought. She would

have to be careful that she didn't allow him to outplay her.

"Your story will be good for the magazine, which is good for me. And it will be great for you, too. You're releasing a new game soon. More exposure equals more sales, right?"

"Yes, a win-win for both of us," he said.

She certainly hoped so.

* * *

The Crystal Terrace was just what Andrea had expected. Set on the top floor in a building on Fisherman's Wharf, the dining room had a gorgeous view of the bay including the infamous island prison of Alcatraz and the iconic Golden Gate Bridge. The décor was warm and luxurious with gleaming hardwood floors, floor-to-ceiling windows and amazing crystal chandeliers.

There wasn't an entrée on the menu under thirty-five dollars, with one steak going for eighty-two dollars. She couldn't imagine what would make a piece of meat worth that much money, but then again, she was more of a cheeseburger-kind-of-girl. Apparently, Alex Donovan was not. He'd shown no hesitancy ordering expensive wine, a sampler of gourmet appetizers and a lobster dish that looked amazing. She'd gone for the filet mignon, figuring she might as well take advantage of the rare opportunity to dine like a celebrity.

Alex had obviously visited the restaurant on many occasions. The waiters greeted him by name, and he was treated with enormous courtesy and respect. A few other diners stopped by their table to say a quick hello, each giving her a rather curious look. She wasn't surprised by their interest; she doubted she was the kind of woman Alex usually took out to dinner.

She sipped her wine as Alex finished his meal. So far, their conversation had been fairly inconsequential. She'd learned that Alex liked movies, especially science fiction, ran at least three times a week, enjoyed sports, rooted for the local teams and had played some baseball when he was a kid. She'd also discovered that while his charm came easy, hard answers were more difficult to come by—not that she'd really pressed him yet. She'd wanted to give him time to warm up to her, but he was going to be guarded no matter how much time she gave him.

"So," she began.

"So," he echoed, meeting her gaze.

She smiled. "This doesn't have to be painful."

"Not for you."

"Let's talk about your company. How did you get into making games? Were you a big gamer as a child?"

"Yes. I've always enjoyed games. The more challenging the better. As technology evolved, so has the way the world plays games. We've gone from simple board games to computer games, video games, virtual reality experiences and mobile apps that allow people to play wherever they are. They don't need friends for these games, they can play alone or with anyone in the world in a multi-player digital online game."

She heard the passion in his voice. There was no doubt that Alex's business was more than just a moneymaker. It was something he believed in. She admired a man who pursued his goals with intensity and determination. Still, he was making games...

"Wouldn't some people argue that your games encourage children to spend far too many hours inside, hooked up to electronics, when they should be experiencing the real world?" she asked.

A smile played around his lips. "Would one of those persons be at this table? Do you not like games, Andrea?"

"I like games," she said defensively. "And you haven't answered my question."

"I would argue that for many of my customers, games connect them to the world. My team works hard to create games that are educational as well as entertaining."

"What about the violence in video games?"

"There's violence in the real world, too, but in games you have control."

She thought about his words, wondering about the undercurrent in his voice, what he wasn't saying…

When he didn't continue speaking, she moved on. "How did you get started? I know you were a millionaire by age twenty-five, so I assume your vision started a lot earlier."

"I started making up games when I was in elementary school. By the time I was a teenager, I had sketched out rough illustrations of multiple worlds. But it was all just a very big and impossible dream back then. I didn't grow up in a world of opportunity, so I had to find my own way into the industry. I started out working in an arcade at a miniature golf course. In between selling tokens and cleaning up after birthday parties, I was doing research. I had access to the database of some of the games. I could see which games were the most popular, the most challenging and who played them. Some were geared more to girls, others to boys. I made notes and files, thinking some day I would use them."

"How did that day come?" she asked curiously. "It's a big leap to go from working in an arcade to running a million—or is it a billion—dollar company?"

"We've done well," he said. "As for the leap, I took a job at a game company."

"Were you really a janitor there?"

"I see you already know the answer."

"I only had about an hour to prep for this dinner, so I don't know that much, and I'd prefer to hear your story from you."

"I was hired as part of the cleaning crew, yes. I wanted to be in that industry and that was the only job I was qualified to do. Three months in, I became friendly with one of the tech guys. He let me sit with him when I was off work. I learned a lot in those sessions, and it was his mentoring that encouraged me to take some computer programming classes at the local community college. Soon I was giving him ideas, and he was creating them. The ideas turned out to be winners, and eventually the head of the company took notice. He gave me a real job on the development team, and that's when my career took off."

"How old were you then?"

"Nineteen."

"That's impressive. How long did you stay with that company?"

"Three years. At twenty-two, I wanted to launch my own game. I quit and created my own company. That tech guy became the head of my development team."

"So the mentor becomes your employee?"

"More like my partner. Cameron is brilliant and he now runs a staff of thirty-seven developers located around the world."

"And how many people does your company employ worldwide?"

"At last report, we were around three hundred and twenty-five employees."

She really wished she wasn't so impressed with his story, but he certainly had created an empire from very little. "Tell me about your family. I know that your parents were killed in a car crash when you were twelve. What happened to you after that?"

"I bounced around the system for a few months until they located my aunt. She took me in, and I lived with her until she died. When she passed away, I was eighteen and almost done with high school, so the foster system was not interested in me; I was on my own."

"That's sad," she murmured.

A curtain had come down over his gaze, and she couldn't read his expression at all now.

"It was a long time ago. To be frank, I'd prefer not to relive my past. A lot of people in this world have difficult childhoods. I'm not unusual in that regard. I think it's more important to focus on the present and the future."

"I can understand that. But my profile is about you, the man, and where you come from is important."

"I just told you where I come from. There's nothing else to say."

She seriously doubted that, but she could see by his stiffening jaw that she was not going to get anything more out of him right now. So she would drop it—for the moment. She looked down at her empty plate and stabbed her fork at the last roasted potato. With that gone, she leaned over to spear an errant carrot on Alex's plate.

His hand came down on her wrist in a harsh, unyielding grip. "Don't."

She looked at him in amazement, the intensity in his voice catching her completely off guard. "I'm sorry. Were you going to eat that?"

"Yes."

A look came into his eyes that made her catch her breath. Finally, there was emotion in those green eyes, and pain—a remembrance of something old, something that must have hurt him deeply. She didn't know what to say. His reaction was so out of character and in such ridiculous proportion to her meaningless act.

She cleared her throat, trying to ease the tension in his face. "Can I have my hand back if I promise not to trespass again?"

Alex looked down at her wrist trapped in the grip of his hand. He quickly released her. "I'm sorry. If you're still hungry, we can order something more. They make an excellent chocolate mousse here. Or carrot cake, that's always been my favorite."

Andrea waited for him to stop talking, and her silence forced him to look into her eyes. "Are you all right?" she asked.

"I'm fine. Do you want something else to eat?"

"No."

"Then I'll get the check." He motioned for the waiter to come over, then handed him his credit card. "Tomorrow, I've made plans for you to see how I spend my weekends. You'll also be able to meet some of my friends."

"All right." She wished she could get him talk about his strange reaction a moment earlier, but there was something about his gaze that told her that line of questioning wouldn't get her anywhere.

"I'll pick you up in the morning—around ten," he said. "Will that be all right?"

"I'd like to see where you live. Why don't I meet you at your place?"

"Fine."

He gave her the address, and she jotted it down on her phone.

"Do you know the area?" he asked.

"No, but should I just look for the biggest mansion on the block?"

"It's large, but not quite the biggest."

"You mean there are still a few goals left for Alexander Donovan to accomplish?"

"A few." He let out a breath as the tension eased from his face. "What about you, Andrea? What kind of goals do you have for yourself?"

"I want to do my job well."

"No bigger dream? What about winning a Pulitzer prize?"

"I wouldn't say no to that, but it's probably an unrealistic and impossible goal."

"Most worthy goals are filled with challenges. When did you decide to be a reporter?"

"When I was ten years old. I started the first fifth-grade newspaper at Hazelton Elementary School. It was one page, and I handed it out at recess."

"Fifth grade. You were an early achiever. What did you write about?"

"My first story was about why they moved the garbage cans to the other side of the playground," she replied, smiling at the memory.

"Was that an important move?"

"Not at all, but I wanted something to write about, and that was the only thing I could think of." She paused. "My father was a foreign correspondent. He traveled all over the world reporting on wars, politics, famine and global changes. I grew up hearing from him about the power of the press to change the world, and I wanted to follow in his footsteps."

"He sounds like an admirable man."

"He made a difference by revealing truths that needed to be told. I wanted to be just like him. Unfortunately, I soon realized that the power of the press can be squashed by those in actual power."

"How so?"

"When the principal at my elementary school decided that girls couldn't play flag football with the boys, I wrote an article about discrimination and passed it around the school."

"I'm surprised you knew how to spell discrimination," he said with a grin.

"I did have to look it up. But I've always been an excellent speller."

"What happened?"

"The principal gave me detention for a week and made me

write, 'I'll mind my own business' five thousand times. It was very unfair. I wanted to write about that injustice but my mother told me she would ground me for a month if I did. She didn't like her daughter being a troublemaker."

"It doesn't appear to me that you learned your lesson very well, since you're still sticking your nose into other people's business."

"But now other people's business *is* my business. And I don't back down from challenges. If the story is important, I go after it, regardless of the potential fall-out. The public has a right to know."

Alex settled back in his seat. "I'm not sure I agree with the public having the right to know everything. What about personal privacy?"

"I'm not against personal privacy," she said carefully. "But you're a public figure, Alex. You've made yourself that. So I think you have to accept the fact that you have less privacy than someone like me. And if you're really concerned about your privacy, why did you agree to the interview?"

"That's a good question. I don't mind sharing my insights on my business and to a certain extent my life, my philosophy and my future goals. I understand that my story can inspire others, but what I don't understand is why anyone would care whether I squeeze my toothpaste from the top or the bottom or where was the most interesting place I've had sex."

"You've been talking to entertainment reporters."

"Too many," he agreed.

"So what were your answers to those questions? Toothpaste, top or bottom? Sex?" She paused, thinking she was probably a little too interested in his answer. She wasn't an entertainment reporter, and she didn't need to know the answers for her article. But she was suddenly very curious.

Alex grinned. "I don't think my bulldog comment earlier was too far off the mark. You're going to make this difficult for me, aren't you, Andrea?"

"Not if you tell me what I want to know."

"What about what I want?" he asked, a sparkle in his eyes.

She caught her breath. "What do you want?"

"Maybe I want to know the most interesting place you've had sex."

He leaned forward, and she found herself doing the same, impulsively wishing there wasn't a table between them, because she suddenly felt an incredibly intense pull to this man.

"Well?" he pressed.

She couldn't even remember the question. She just knew it had something to do with sex. And thinking about sex and Alex Donovan in the same moment made her palms sweat.

Then the waiter interrupted.

"Your check, sir." The crisp words caught them both off guard.

Andrea sat back in her seat. Alex did the same.

The waiter pushed the booklet toward Alex and stood patiently by the table.

"Oh, of course," Alex replied.

As Alex busied himself with signing the credit card receipt, Andrea blew out a breath and tried to calm her racing pulse. She felt both relieved and frustrated by the interruption. For a second there, she'd thought Alex was going to lean across the table and kiss her. Worse—she'd wanted him to, and that was a reckless thought.

She drew in a deep breath as her phone began to buzz. She pulled it out of her bag and checked the number—it was her sister. She couldn't answer the call now, but she knew she really needed to touch base with Laurel. While she might be able to get away with being a bad bridesmaid, she couldn't be a bad sister.

"Work?" Alex quizzed.

"No," she said, putting the phone away. "My sister Laurel. She's getting married in a couple of weeks, and I have been falling a little short on my maid-of-honor duties."

"Do you need to talk to her?"

"I'll touch base with her later. She's going out tonight with some of our friends, so I'm sure she'll be fine until tomorrow."

"Is she older or younger?"

"We're twins."

"That's interesting."

"I suppose. It's all I've ever known."

"And you're close?"

"Very close. We've always done everything together: school, soccer, a short stint in gymnastics, until we both realized we were more likely to break something than win any awards."

Alex smiled. "It sounds like you're alike."

"Actually, we're very different, opposites in almost every way, but we're still super close, which has always amazed our friends. We went to college together, and we're part of a really tight group of girlfriends, who are all going to be bridesmaids in Laurel's wedding." She stopped abruptly, realizing she was rambling, but she was still rattled by her almost kiss with Alexander Donovan. "You don't want to hear all this."

"I'd rather talk about you than me."

"I'm not surprised, but we do need to keep talking about you."

"We will—tomorrow."

"It's still early," she protested.

"I have to meet someone," he said.

Of course he did. He probably had a real date waiting. "I understand."

"Maybe you can catch up with your friends."

"Maybe," she said lightly.

"Shall we go?"

"Lead the way."

* * *

Alex rolled down the window of his Mercedes as he drove away from the restaurant, feeling hot and a little off his game, and it was all because of Andrea. She was not what he'd expected. Not only was she a pretty blonde, but she was smart as hell, and he would not be able to pull his usual bullshit on her. He was both intrigued and annoyed by that realization. It had been a long time since he'd met a woman who challenged him in any way. But he needed to remember that Andrea had only one goal and that was to get him to spill his secrets. Her only interest in him was what he could do for her career.

Maybe it was good that her motives were in the open. He'd had women try to get ahead by getting involved with him. At least Andrea wasn't trying to hide anything.

But that didn't mean he was going to give her a good story. As far as he was concerned, by the end of this weekend she wouldn't know much more about him than she knew right now. And she would write an article like all the others he'd done.

"Where are we going tomorrow?" Andrea asked, as he pulled up in front of his office building, so she could get her car.

"You'll see."

"Really? You can't even give me a straight answer about that?" she asked dryly.

He grinned. "I like to be mysterious. But I will say that we're going to do something I enjoy very much." He gave her a quick glance. "Don't look so worried. It's not X-rated."

"I'm not worried. I can handle anything you have planned."

"That's probably true." He paused. "You didn't ask for this

story, did you?"

"No," she admitted. "But it doesn't matter. I'm committed to doing a good job."

"What story would you rather be working on?"

"The one I've been researching the past six weeks."

"What's it about?"

"I can't get into details, but I have located a possible whistleblower in a company that makes something important to a lot of people. Something that if it isn't done right could be life-threatening."

He was intrigued by her words. "Now who's being mysterious?"

She shrugged. "I can't say more until I have more."

"So why did you take this assignment? It sounds like you have a much better story in the works."

"A story that is taking too long to pan out. My boss needs me to earn my paycheck." She sighed. "I really shouldn't have told you that."

"Your secret is safe with me."

She stared back at him. "Thank you. I wish I could say the same, but—"

"But anything I say is fair game, got it."

"I must admit I'm more interested in your story now that you've told me a little about your past. You have done some amazing things, Alex. I can't wait to hear more."

"You will. Where are you parked?"

"Over there. The red Scion."

"Ah, red. It suits you."

"I don't think you know me well enough to know that."

"I'm getting a pretty good picture, and a person's car says something about their style and personality."

"Then why do you drive a black Mercedes? It seems rather dull for someone the press has called the 'King of Games'."

"You're right. I do have other vehicles, but this is the car I use to impress serious reporters," he said with a grin.

"I'm glad you consider me a serious reporter. So what do you really drive?"

"I have a Jeep that I use for pleasure. I take it up in the mountains and there's no place I can't go. It gives me complete and absolute freedom. Maybe I'll give you a ride sometime."

"Sounds like fun. We could do that tomorrow."

"No, tomorrow's plans are set."

"Fine, we'll play it your way, but you know you don't have to spend time impressing me. I just want to know the real you."

He could have said that only one or two people in his life knew the real him, but that would only give her another clue to latch onto, and he was trying to give her just enough detail to satisfy her curiosity and no more. "I'll see you tomorrow, Andrea. Don't be late."

"I'm never late," she said quickly, then she uttered a little laugh. "Actually, that's not true. I'm often late, because I try to do a dozen things all at the same time, but tomorrow I will be at your house at ten."

"Good," he said. "Because unlike you, I am always on time."

She tipped her head in acknowledgement, then got out of the car. He watched her walk down the street, enjoying the way the moonlight bounced off her blonde waves and the sexy swing of her hips. His body tightened as alarm bells went off in his mind. Letting this reporter follow him around all weekend might just be the biggest mistake he'd made in a long time.

Chapter Three

Saturday morning, Andrea woke up to the ring of the doorbell. It took her a second to react. She'd been up half the night doing research on Alex Donovan, not falling asleep until nearly dawn. Rolling out of bed in pajama bottoms and a t-shirt, she looked through the peephole and saw her sister. Opening the door, she said. "What are you doing here so early?"

"I figured this was the best time to catch you." Laurel handed Andrea a coffee. "You look like you could use this."

"I definitely can," she said, thinking some caffeine might clear the haze out of her head.

As Laurel entered her small apartment, Andrea's cell phone began to ring. "Why is everyone up so early?" she muttered, grabbing her phone. She groaned as she saw her mother's name on the screen. "It's Mom."

"Better get it. She'll just keep calling," Laurel said, sitting down on the couch.

"Hi, Mom."

"What took you so long to answer the phone?" her mom asked. "You weren't still asleep, were you?"

She glanced at the clock, surprised that it was eight-thirty. She was normally up by seven. "I was working late last night. What's up?"

"I want to talk to you about Laurel's bridal shower. You told me that if I sent out the invitations, you would do the rest, but it's in two weeks, and I haven't heard a word from you."

"I know, I'm sorry," she quickly apologized. "But I can't talk about it right now. Can I call you later, or maybe tomorrow? I have a meeting today."

"A meeting with the sexy millionaire?" her mom asked.

She frowned. "Who told you about that?"

"Kate. She came by the house to pick up Laurel for drinks yesterday."

"Great," she muttered.

"So how was your date?"

"It wasn't a date, it was a dinner meeting."

"Fine, but you still haven't told me if you had a good time."

"The food was excellent. Alex was interesting."

"It's already Alex?"

She heard the hopeful note in her mother's voice and knew she needed to squelch it. "Mom, you're making too much of this."

"He's single, isn't he?"

"As far as I know."

"Are you meeting him again today?"

"I am," she admitted.

"Wear something nice, Andrea."

"I'm not out to impress the man, I'm trying to interview him."

"It doesn't hurt to look good," Sandra Blain replied. "Alexander Donovan would be a very good catch."

"I'm not trying to catch him. He's not my type."

"A handsome millionaire isn't your type?" her mother asked in astonishment. "What is wrong with you?"

"Nothing. He's a player, Mom. All those guys are."

"He might not be."

"You're always such an optimist when it comes to men."

"And you're a pessimist."

She had good reason to be.

"I ran into Douglas the other day," her mom continued. "He and Cassie just had a baby."

"Great." The last person she wanted to talk about was her ex-boyfriend.

"They seem quite happy together. But I still think he should have married you."

"Well, he didn't. And if you want grandchildren, I'd work on Laurel." She grinned at her sister, who stuck her tongue out at her. "I really have to go, Mom."

"Just give Alexander Donovan a chance," her mother pleaded.

"The only thing I want from Alexander Donovan is a good cover story that will take my career to the next level."

"You and your career," her mom said with a sigh. "You're just like your father. I never understood him, and I never seem to understand you."

"Well, at least you have one daughter you do understand," she said lightly, feeling a little pain at her mom's words. "I'll talk to you later."

She ended the call and tossed her phone down on the coffee table.

"Mom called you about the bridal shower, didn't she?" Laurel asked with a knowing smile.

She smiled back at her twin. She and Laurel were fraternal twins, and while they loved each other to death, they looked nothing alike. Laurel had brown hair and blue eyes and was three inches taller and quite a bit bustier. Laurel was also a girly girl. She loved make-up, clothes, going shopping and having parties. While she enjoyed her job as a recruiter for a tech company, she was much more interested in her upcoming wedding and her plans for marriage and a family with her soon-to-be husband Greg than she was in her job.

Andrea took a sip of her coffee as she sat down in the chair across from Laurel. "Mom is worried that I'm not going to plan your shower."

"Well, you're not, are you?" Laurel asked, giving her a pointed glance. "I figured you were going to let Mom do it."

"She'll do it whether I want her to do it or not, but I should get more involved. It's not that I don't want to. I want you to have the perfect shower, bachelorette party, wedding— the whole shebang. I know I've been a little crazed with work, but I promise to put all of your events on the front burner as soon as I get through this weekend of interviews."

"I'm not worried."

"Really? Then why are you here so early in the morning?"

"I wanted to ask you something."

The serious note in her sister's voice surprised her. "Okay. Go ahead."

"Do you think I'm crazy for marrying Greg without having had a few more serious relationships?"

"You're having doubts about Greg?" she asked slowly, taken aback by the question. Laurel had been in love with Greg since their first date six years ago.

"The doubts are more about me. I'm twenty-seven years old, and I've been with Greg since I was twenty-one. I haven't been single in the city like you and the rest of our friends. Sometimes I listen to everyone's dating adventure stories and wonder if I'm missing out."

"Of course you're missing out. You're missing out on a lot of losers. It's not all that great to be single, Laurel." She paused. "What's really the problem?"

"I don't know," she said with a sigh. "I just feel jittery. And for some reason when Kate told me you were going out with a sexy billionaire, I felt kind of—jealous."

"It wasn't a date. It was an interview. You're all making

this out to be more than it is. And I think you and Greg are perfect together. He wants everything you want. He accepts you for who you are. And he's a good man with a good heart. Plus, you've been hot for him since your first date."

"That's true. I'm being stupid, aren't I?"

"You are. But I'm you're sister, and I will stand by you no matter what you decide. I'll even drive the getaway car if you can't make it down the aisle at the last minute."

"Mom would die if I ran out on my wedding."

"That's very true, but it's your life, not hers."

Laurel met her gaze. "You're a good sister—horrible at being a maid of honor, but really good at everything else."

"I'll do better," she promised. "So the wedding is still on?"

Laurel nodded. "It's on."

"Great. I need to take a shower, so…"

"I'm going. I have a bunch of errands to run. I have to find a new wedding photographer."

"Why? I thought all those plans were made."

"The one I had signed up is now pregnant and suffering horrendous morning sickness. Mom doesn't want to take a chance that she might not feel well the day of my wedding."

"I guess I see her point."

"Kate has been trying to get me a sub from her list of photographers, but everyone is booked so close to the date. I talked to Liz, and she has a few photographers she's worked with at her P.R. agency, so she set up some meetings for me today."

Kate was not only a bridesmaid but also Laurel's official wedding planner. Still, Andrea felt a twinge of guilt that Laurel had had to turn to not only Kate but also Liz for help. Liz was one of the bridesmaids, but she wasn't the maid of honor. "I could probably ask the guy who shoots for the magazine. He might have some contacts who do weddings."

"I may take you up on that," Laurel replied as she got to

her feet. "But let me see what happens today."

"Okay," she said, following her sister to the door. "How is Liz doing? I haven't spoken to her in a few weeks. I know her dad hasn't been well."

"Unfortunately, he's still not well. Liz is trying to take over his responsibilities at the firm, but it's a lot of work, and I guess her father's partners are giving her crap. They're figuring that her dad will be out soon, and they'd just as soon get her out, too."

"But Liz's dad founded that company."

"He had some sort of falling out with his partners. Liz is caught in the middle. Her dad wants her to take over his part of the partnership, but the other men don't want that."

"That sounds horrible." She made a mental note to call Liz later and catch up.

Laurel paused at the door. "I know you're going to do whatever you want, Andrea, but I just have to say one thing…"

"What's that?" she asked warily.

"It wouldn't kill you to give Alex Donovan a chance to be something more than an interview subject, Andrea."

"Alex doesn't want that chance. He just wants me to write a fluff piece about his life, and I have no intention of doing that. I need to make this story good. My job is kind of on the line."

"Really?" Laurel asked in surprise. "But you always work so hard."

"Unfortunately, I haven't had a lot of results to show for that work. But I have a cover story now, and I'm going to make the most of it. I'm going to find out who Alex Donovan really is, whatever it takes."

"Maybe the real Alex Donovan will be even more interesting than the one the rest of the world knows."

"I would love to be that lucky."

* * *

An hour later, Andrea rang the doorbell to Alex's impressive Victorian mansion in Pacific Heights. It was a far cry from her small one-bedroom apartment in the Sunset, but she didn't care. While she liked money as much as anyone else, she was more interested in doing something that would influence people and the way they thought about the world, not that this piece would do anything more than raise the blood pressure of American women everywhere.

With a sigh, she pushed the button again.

Alex opened the door with a cheerful smile. He wore tan slacks and short-sleeved cream-colored polo shirt. He looked just as good in casual attire as he had in the suit he'd had on the night before.

"You're right on time," he said.

"As ordered."

"Come in." He held the door open for her, and Andrea walked into the impressive entryway. The floor was marble title. Oil paintings adorned the walls, and an enormous staircase curved around a pillar as it rose up to the second floor.

"Wow," she muttered. "Nice digs."

He grinned. "You haven't seen the rest of the house."

"I doubt I'll be disappointed. Can I have a tour?"

"Another time. We need to leave now to meet my friends."

"Are you sure we don't have a few moments?" She was itching to take a look around his personal space, because nothing about the front rooms seemed remotely personal. Off to one side, the living room was in shadows, but she could see the same kind of luxurious furniture and art through the archway.

"Don't worry. You'll have a chance to see the house later."
He opened the front door, and she followed him out to the
circular drive where his Mercedes was waiting.

"Where are we going?" she asked, as she got into the
passenger seat.

"A small party some friends of mine are throwing."

"That's rather vague. At some point, the two of us need to
sit down and talk privately."

"Of course."

"So, do you live alone?" she asked, as he pulled out of the
driveway.

"I do."

"No live-in staff?"

He shook his head. "I have a cleaning service that comes
in once a week, and a personal chef that makes meals for me
when I'm going to be home."

She wasn't surprised to hear that. Still she couldn't help
wondering how fun it was to live in such a big house all alone.

"What about you?" he asked. "Where do you live?"

"I have a one-bedroom apartment in the Sunset. I moved
in about three months ago, and I'm excited to have my own
place. While I've loved all my roommates, I've been living
with different women for the past eight years, and I shared my
last apartment with four women. It was a little too chaotic."

"It sounds crazy. I can't imagine."

She doubted he could imagine. His life was quite different
from hers. "My entire apartment would probably fit into your
living room. Don't you ever feel a little lost living in a
mansion by yourself? How many bedrooms are there?"

"Six. I have visitors, but like you, I also prefer to be on
my own."

"You've never had a woman move in with you?"

"That's a personal question," he returned.

"Well, I'm a reporter. I ask personal questions."

"No."

"That's it?" she prodded.

"You asked, I answered."

"Elaboration always makes for a better article."

"Then ask a more interesting question."

She sighed. Alex Donovan was definitely not going to make this easy. As he turned down the next block, she realized they were heading toward the Marina, and memories of a fateful fourth-grade fishing trip flashed through her mind. "We're not going out on a boat, are we?" she asked.

He turned into the harbor parking lot. "We are. My friend has a beautiful yacht. You'll love it."

She was absolutely sure she would not love it. But she couldn't back out of the trip now. She wouldn't have too many chances to talk to Alex, and she only had ten days to put the story together.

After he parked the car, she got out and met him on the sidewalk. There was a brisk wind, which did not make her feel any better about the upcoming trip.

Alex gave her a sharp look as she zipped her jacket. "Are you okay?"

"Fine," she said with determination. She told herself she wasn't ten years old anymore and sailing on a yacht would be nothing like going out in a small fishing boat.

Two hours later she knew it was worse.

* * *

While the yacht was massive in size, it was no match for the wind-driven waves that lifted the boat up and down in joyful glee. The first hour had been okay. Andrea had concentrated on getting to know Alex's friends, and the party of twenty had remained docked at the pier with several waiters passing out appetizers and champagne.

Everything had changed when they sailed out into the bay, gliding slowly along the shoreline, taking a good view of Alcatraz Island before heading out for the turbulent ocean waters on the other side of the Golden Gate Bridge. She'd come out on the deck fifteen minutes earlier, desperately needing some air to quell the queasiness, but being outside wasn't really any better. Along with feeling like she might throw up, she was now a little concerned that she might also get tossed off the boat.

A splash of water hit her in the face as the boat came down at a particularly vicious angle, and she held on to the rail in a death grip. She didn't know how everyone else was doing it, but all she could hear from down below was music and laugher. The rest of the party seemed able to maintain their balance while eating liver pate and munching on sculpted vegetables.

"Andrea. You look..." Alex paused by her side, studying her face with genuine concern. "You're green. I've heard people described that way, but I've never actually seen it before."

"Thanks for the update." She pushed her hair out of her face in a futile gesture. A second later, the wind whipped the damp strands that had escaped from her ponytail across her eyes.

"Maybe you need some food," Alex suggested.

She groaned. "Don't even mention food to me."

"Sorry." He put an arm around her shoulders, steadying her as the boat rocked back and forth. "It's rougher than usual today."

"Is it? The last time I was on a boat I was ten, and it felt very much like this. Only then I threw up all over Johnny Carmichael's tennis shoes." She took a breath as bile rose in her throat. "You might want to back up."

"I'll take my chances," he said with a small smile. "You

should have told me you get seasick. Why didn't you?"

She sent him an irritated look. "Following you around is my job. I go where the story goes. And I was hoping I'd outgrown it. But I'll be fine. I just need to breathe." She tightened her grip on the rail as the boat took another dive. "How much longer are we going to be out here?"

"We're heading back now, but it will probably be another twenty minutes before we dock."

"Okay. Twenty minutes. I can handle that." She silently repeated the words, trying to will the nausea out of her stomach.

Alex rubbed her shoulder with his hand. "Your muscles are super tight."

"You're a master of stating the obvious. This doesn't bother you at all, does it?" she asked, casting a quick look into his amused eyes.

"No, I love the feel of the waves. Maybe you should come downstairs."

She shook her head. "I'm staying right here. If I do throw up, I won't have any witnesses, especially if you go back to your friends."

"I'm not going to leave you alone."

She was both happy and dismayed by his answer. While she appreciated the company, she liked to be professional when she was on the job, and right now she felt anything but professional. And it wasn't just the ocean that was bothering her; it was Alex. He was so close to her she could smell the scent of his aftershave. The scent didn't turn her stomach. In fact, it made her want to curl into his side, rest her head on his chest, which would be completely inappropriate. What the hell was wrong with her?

"So who at this party are you really close to?" she asked, desperately trying to find something else to think about.

"I know most everyone, except for a few of the dates."

"It's obvious everyone likes you, but who knows the man and not the 'King of Games'?"

"There's no difference."

"I think there is."

"Well, you don't know me well enough to make that assumption."

"I'm trying to get to know you better."

"Do you ever have doubts about your job?" he asked, changing the subject.

"What do you mean?"

"Do you think about the impact your stories might have on someone's life?"

"I always think about the impact. I want to write articles that encourage people to think, that inspire change, that make a difference. If I didn't want to make an impact, I wouldn't be a very good reporter."

"Sometimes reporters cross ethical lines."

"I've never done that."

"Maybe you've never had to make that choice."

She thought about that. "I suppose that's possible."

"If you're so interested in covering stories that make a difference to the world, then you're definitely wasting your time with me."

"You're an important man, not only because of your business but also because of your philanthropy. You are making a difference in the world, and that's the side of you I want to focus on, so you really don't have to keep trying to impress me with your celebrity lifestyle."

"Do you think that's what I'm doing?"

"I'm pretty sure," she said, tightening her grip on the rail as the boat took another serious dive. "Oh, my God, this is crazy."

"Don't look at the water, look at me," he ordered.

It wasn't that easy to tear her gaze away from the sea, but

she finally managed to focus on his face, on his beautiful green eyes. He really was a gorgeous man, she thought, especially now with his dark hair damp from the sea breeze, his eyes sparkling, and his skin reddened by the sun and the wind. He was in his element, and she was—not. She hated to be at a disadvantage, but there was no denying that's exactly where she was now.

"Better?" he asked.

"Not really."

"You need a distraction." His hand slid from her shoulder to her waist, as he moved around in front of her.

She couldn't step away from him without taking her hands off the rail and that was not an option.

He gave her a warm smile. "You're a beautiful woman, Andrea."

"And you are a charming liar."

"You should learn how to take a compliment."

"I'm a mess," she protested.

"That's not what I see."

"Well, then you're blind. And I don't believe this sudden interest in me. I am not your type."

"What do you think is my type?" he asked curiously.

"Blonde, big breasts, fun to party with, and not looking for anything serious—kind of like at least six of the women downstairs. Tell me I'm wrong."

"You are blonde," he said, his grin broadening.

If she hadn't been so determined to hang on to the rail, she might have instinctively put her arms across her breasts, because Alex's curious gaze had dropped to her chest, and at his look, a shiver went down her spine.

Then he lifted his gaze to hers. He shifted his weight, moving a little closer, until there wasn't much more than a breath between them.

"What—what are you doing?" she asked, feeling both

shock and anticipation.

"I'm thinking about kissing you."

"Why?"

"Does there have to be a reason?" he challenged. "I like you. You like me. There's chemistry between us."

"No, there's not," she denied, even though her heart was beating way too fast.

"I think there is."

"Well, even if there was, this story is important to me. I am not going to mess it up by getting involved with you."

"How could a kiss mess anything up?"

She swallowed hard. She couldn't think straight with the turbulent sea rocking the boat and Alex's irresistible smile making her feel completely off balance.

"It's only a matter of time, Andrea. I've known that since the first minute we met."

"When you insulted me with that bulldog comment?"

"I don't think I was wrong. You have definite bulldog tendencies."

She made a face at him. "Well, I don't mix business with pleasure."

"It would be a pleasure." His hands slid around her waist, pulling her into his chest. "Say yes."

She wanted to say yes, but the predatory gleam in his eyes made her realize that this moment was about more than a kiss; it was also a power play. Alex was a gamer. He created battles and adventures for fun and profit, and to do that successfully he had to be a master at reading people, seeing their strengths, their weaknesses, understanding their motivations and using their desires against them. But this wasn't a game. This was her job. And even though every nerve ending in her body was tingling, she found some willpower. "No."

Surprise flashed through his eyes. "Seriously?"

"Your moves aren't going to work on me. This isn't a

game. I'm here with you because it's my job. Neither of us should forget that."

He stared back at her, his gaze reflective, a bit confused, but there was also a hint of respect. "Okay."

She waited for him to elaborate, but he seemed content to hold her, to look at her, which might have been an even better move on his part, because now that he wasn't pressing for a kiss, she found herself wanting him to make that move.

Or maybe she would. How crazy was that?

She licked her lips, swallowed hard, trying to resist the attraction that sizzled around them. She couldn't remember feeling so lit-up, so on-edge. The only good thing was that Alex had definitely taken her mind off the swirling sea.

"Second thoughts?" he asked with a hint of amusement, his intense gaze reading her too well.

"You should let me go," she said finally, her voice a little too breathless. "Go downstairs—see your friends."

"I told you I won't leave you alone up here."

She drew in a breath, turning her head, hoping to see the harbor just seconds away, but they were still off shore.

"No escape route," he said.

"Stop reading my mind."

The boat took another lurch, and she stumbled against him. His arms tightened around her.

"The universe is trying to tell you something," he said lightly, his breath warming her cheek.

It certainly was. She was having enough trouble fighting her own attraction, much less his, and now the ocean had to get in on it.

And then another long dive changed everything as a huge wave broke over the boat, soaking them both in icy water. She gasped, her heart skipping a beat at the shocking spray. She looked at Alex. He appeared just as bewildered as he wiped water from his eyes.

Then his gaze turned to her and he started to laugh. "I guess the universe is on your side after all."

"They do say Mother Nature is a woman."

"I have no doubt about that," he said dryly. "We should go downstairs and dry off. You're going to freeze up here.

"I'll take the cold over the nausea any day, but you go ahead."

He shook his head. "We'll stay close, keep each other warm."

She sighed as he moved closer. Maybe the universe wasn't on her side after all.

Chapter Four

An hour later, Andrea jumped off the yacht with overwhelming relief. She was so happy she almost kissed the ground, but she'd already embarrassed herself enough as it was. She muttered some quick goodbyes to Alex's friends, who seemed even more curious about her relationship with Alex after seeing them both descend from the upper deck in wet clothes. But at this moment, she didn't care what anyone thought. She'd dried off since the ocean had given them both a cold shower, but she was still cold and a little queasy. She just wanted to get dry and warm and hope her stomach would settle down.

After getting in the car, Alex turned the heat on high and sent her a quick look. "Feeling better?"

"Immensely."

"You're getting the color back in your face."

She pulled down the visor and was horrified at the way her tangled, damp hair was falling out of her ponytail. She pulled out her hairband and ran her hand through her hair, which didn't do much to improve her appearance. There was more pink in her cheeks now, but the little makeup she'd had on was completely gone. She did not look at all like any of the other women who'd left the party in the same condition in which they'd arrived.

"Checking the damage?" Alex asked. "You don't look that bad."

"The mirror says otherwise. But I am happy that at least I didn't throw up on you."

"I'm happy about that, too."

She put the visor back up and settled in her seat as the heat finally began to stop her shivers. "Are we going back to your house?"

"Yeah. I'll drop you off at your car."

"I was hoping we might have time to talk or that you could give me a tour of your home."

"Sorry, but I have an appointment. We'll talk later at the cocktail reception for the mayor."

"Another party?"

"You wanted to see how I live. This is what I do on the weekends," he said with a shrug.

"Actually, I want to get to know you, not just follow you around. Is there any way you can postpone what you're doing this afternoon?"

"I'm afraid not."

Frustration ran through her. "You can pretend that letting me tag along at parties is doing an interview, but we both know it isn't. If you didn't want to tell your story, you shouldn't have agreed to be the cover story."

"I've certainly had second thoughts about that in the past twenty-four hours."

"Do you want to pull out? If you do, you better say so now, because the magazine is up against a tight deadline."

"No, I honor my commitments," he said, shooting her a look as he stopped the car at a light.

"Great. Then let's set up a time to talk, to have a real conversation, either before tonight's party or after. Or we skip the party and meet tomorrow," she said, trying to get their relationship back on a more professional level.

Alex didn't answer right away. In fact, he seemed to be pondering something fairly serious, then he said, "All right. You can come with me now."

"Where are we going?"

"To hell and back."

"What?"

"Hang on."

Alex gunned the motor and with a decided squeal of the tires, he made a sharp right turn and sped down the street. It soon became apparent that they were traveling to the other side of town, to a neighborhood very far from the one in which Alex lived.

* * *

The streets in the area of San Francisco known as the Tenderloin were dark and grimy with homeless people on every corner and an air of poverty and despair. Alex's Mercedes came under scrutiny every time they had to stop at an intersection. Andrea instinctively locked her door at one particularly seedy corner.

The motion brought Alex's gaze to her face. "Not your scene? Do you want me to take you home?"

"No. I'm a reporter. I'm used to following stories wherever they go."

"Even to hell?" he said dryly.

"Where are we really going?"

"You'll see."

He drove down another block, past a liquor store, a pawn shop and a bar boasting ninety-nine cent tacos. It was not the San Francisco of the tourist brochures, the cosmopolitan city where people like Alex Donovan wined and dined in fancy restaurants or on elegant yachts. It was an urban neighborhood suffering from harsh economic realities.

She couldn't imagine where they were going. Maybe Alex was taking a shortcut. It was the only answer that made sense. What business would he have on a street like this?

Eventually, he turned into an alley, the passageway so narrow Andrea thought she could reach out a hand and touch the buildings they were passing. Finally the alley opened up and set back to one side was a parking lot and a dirty white sign that read *To Hell And Back.*

Alex pulled into a spot and cut the engine. Then he waved his hand at the sign. "You thought I was kidding."

"What is this place?"

"For a few weeks a long time ago, it was my home."

"Really?" She was more than a little intrigued by the first personal piece of information he'd revealed.

"Let's go inside."

"All right." She followed him through a large warehouse door. One step into the lobby area told her they had entered a gym. While the outside of the building had been less than stellar, the inside was modern and clean. A teenager with a baseball cap on backwards was typing on a computer behind the counter. He stood up and gave Alex a high five.

"Haven't seen you in a while," the kid said.

"I've been working," Alex replied. "Andrea Blain, meet Sammy Jordan."

"Nice to meet you."

"You, too." He turned to Alex. "Are you looking for some action today?"

"No, I need to see Mick. Is he in his office?"

"He's working the ring."

"Thanks," Alex said, as the boy sat down, returning his attention to his computer.

Alex led her through another set of double doors that led into a large open space. She paused for a moment to take it all in. There were weights and fitness machines on one side of the room, with at least a dozen guys working out. Then there was a large area with nothing but boxing bags hanging from the ceiling. An instructor was showing a kid how to use his legs in a kickboxing maneuver. Finally, there were two glass-walled rooms that appeared to be exercise studios, although there were no classes currently in session.

Alex moved toward the boxing ring where two teenage boys were battling while a middle-aged man oversaw their match. As they walked across the gym, Andrea was more than aware of a few gazes turning in their direction.

"Everyone is looking at us," she murmured. "You must be well-known around here."

He gave her a dry smile. "It's all you, Andrea. Not many women come through those doors."

"So what are we doing here?"

"I need to talk to Mick. He's the owner."

They paused at the edge of the ring. Alex made no move to interrupt the sparring match.

Andrea watched for a moment and then said, "What did you mean when you told me that you lived here a long time ago?"

"It was after my aunt died. I didn't have anywhere to stay, and Mick let me sleep on the couch in his office for a few weeks until I could finish high school. I was going to quit school and get a job, but he wouldn't let me."

"I didn't read about this place in any of the articles you've done previously."

"It never came up."

As Alex finished speaking, Mick came down the stairs. In his early fifties, Mick was built like a linebacker, tall, broad and square. His hair was a dirty blond and cut very short. He wore gym pants and a t-shirt, and she could see numerous tattoos on his arms. The heavy lines around his eyes and mouth hinted at some hard living.

"Alex," Mick said, slapping Alex on the shoulder. "Haven't seen you in a few months. Where have you been hiding?"

"My office mostly," Alex said. "Mick Galliard meet Andrea Blain. Andrea is writing an article about me for *World News Today*. She's shadowing me this week."

"And you brought her here?" Mick asked, surprise in his voice.

The two men exchanged a rather pointed look, then Alex shrugged. "She was in the car."

"Well," Mick replied. "I guess that's a good enough reason." He turned his sharp gaze to Andrea. "It's a pleasure."

"Mine, too," she said, shaking his hand.

Alex pulled an envelope out of his pocket. "I wanted to bring this by for you, Mick."

Mick's lips drew into a line. "That better not be money."

"I talked to Howard. You should have come to me."

"You've done enough already, Alex. This is my business, not yours."

"You're doing good things here, Mick. That's what matters. So put your pride aside. And use this for the kids."

Mick hesitated and then took the envelope and slipped it into his pocket. "Thanks. It's just a loan. I'll pay you back."

"I don't want you to pay me back. As long as you keep getting results, that's all that matters. How is it looking for the next event?"

"I've got an up and coming champion," Mick said, nodding his head to a solidly built older teenager who had just stepped into the ring. "Kyle has strength, speed, agility and smarts. Kind of reminds me of you."

"Of you?" Andrea echoed, giving Alex a questioning look.

"I spent a few hours in the ring."

Mick snorted at that. "More like a few months." Mick

turned to Andrea. "Alex was good. He won a couple of regional events, but while he had all the moves, his heart wasn't in it. He was meant to do a lot more. And he did. Now I have to get back to work. You two going to stick around?"

"For a few minutes," Alex said.

"Don't be a stranger. I know you've got a gym in your house, but we've got some machines here I know you don't have yet."

"I'll keep that in mind."

As Mick went back to the ring to set up the next match, Andrea gave Alex a thoughtful look. "You keep this place going, don't you?"

"Not at all. I just help out every now and then. Mick has been a savior for a lot of kids in this city—kids who can't pay to use a gym. It's an important place in this neighborhood, and I chip in when he needs it."

"He was your savior, too, wasn't he?"

Alex's gaze was serious and reflective. "Definitely one of them."

"Were you really as good a boxer as Mick said?"

He smiled. "I held my own. But what boxing really gave me was confidence, a feeling of power, of being able to take care of myself. Mick teaches these kids a lot more than how to fight. And the boxing ring is a good place to burn off anger and other emotions that can lead kids into trouble."

She thought about that. "Did you have a lot of anger after your parents died?"

"The normal amount."

"You like to be vague. Is that because you don't want to talk to me, or because you just can't talk about those feelings?"

He looked away from the ring to meet her gaze. "Maybe a little of both."

She liked his answer. It felt honest and real for the first time. "I understand."

"You do?"

"I was thirteen when my father died. I still had my mom and my sister, so my situation wasn't at all like yours, but I do know the pain of losing a parent. It's hard to talk about. And I wasn't much older than you."

"It is hard to talk about. I didn't realize, Andrea. I'm sorry for your loss."

"Thanks."

Their gazes clung for a long moment, and a different kind of shiver ran down her spine, one that wasn't just sexual chemistry but an emotional connection.

She cleared her throat, realizing they were getting off track once again. She wasn't supposed to be the one talking; he was. "So tell me more about your time here."

"Not much more to tell. I went to school, worked in the gym, did some boxing, slept on Mick's couch until graduation, and then I moved on."

"To the video arcade and then the tech company?"

"To name two. I had many jobs over a five-year period. I did whatever I could do to make enough money to pay rent to someone, usually friends who offered me their couches for a hundred bucks a month."

"You've certainly come a long way." She was beginning to realize that Alex's rags to riches story was very genuine and would probably inspire a lot of readers once they heard his story. She wondered why he hadn't spoken more about his past in previous interviews. "How come you didn't bring the other reporters here?"

"I prefer to focus on the present and the future."

"But the man you are today has been shaped by your past, and that's interesting."

"We all have pasts. We all have challenges. I don't like it when people use hard times as an excuse or even as a reason why they succeeded. The past becomes a crutch or a stepping stone, but all that really matters is living in the moment, making the right decision, living your life."

She nodded, wishing she'd had her phone recorder on so she could have captured his words. Then again, he probably wouldn't have spoken so freely if she'd been recording or even taking notes.

"We should get going," Alex said. "I have to make a few calls and take care of some work items this afternoon. Then we have the party tonight."

"I'd like to talk to Mick about you, get his perspective on the *Man of the Year*. Would that be possible?"

"Not today. Saturdays are busy. Maybe another time."

"All right." She didn't need Alex to talk to Mick. In fact, she'd probably get more information out of Mick if Alex weren't around.

"That was a little too easy," Alex said as they walked out of the gym.

"What?"

"Your willingness to leave without asking any more questions."

She gave him a smile. "I can always come back."

"I'm going to be sorry I brought you here, aren't I?"

"I don't know. Does Mick have some dirt on you?"

"If he did, he wouldn't tell you."

"Probably true." She'd seen the affection between the men and she had no doubt there was loyalty as well, especially since Alex was supporting the gym financially. But even if Mick couldn't relate any secrets, he could still give her insight into her subject, and the more insight she had, the better questions she could ask Alex.

Chapter Five

Alex drove back to his house feeling restless and a little annoyed with himself for taking Andrea to the gym. But it was too late now. He'd given her a peephole into his past, and he was quite sure she would take advantage of it at the first opportunity.

He pulled into his driveway but didn't bother to shut off the engine. He needed to get back to the gym and talk to Mick.

"You're not going inside?" Andrea asked.

"No, I have to run an errand. I'll pick you up at your place at six, all right?"

"Sounds good. Cocktail attire?"

He nodded, thinking that he'd like to see her in a sexy, short dress.

"This party isn't on a boat or a plane or any other moving vehicle, is it?" she asked.

Smiling, he said, "No, it's in a building, but there is a high-speed elevator to the fiftieth floor. Can you handle that? Because otherwise it's going to be a long walk up the stairs."

She smiled back at him. "Would you walk with me?"

"No way. But I would have a drink waiting when you got to the top."

"I can handle the elevator."

"Good."

She opened her door, then paused, glancing back at him. "Thanks for taking me to the gym. I think I finally caught a brief glimpse of the real you."

"The real me isn't hiding, Andrea. What you see is what you get."

"I don't think that's true at all. Everyone has layers, and I suspect you have quite a few. I'm looking forward to unraveling them."

She got out of the car and shut the door. As he watched her walk to her car, all he could think about was how he'd like to unravel some of her clothes—forget about layers.

Shaking his head, he told himself to get a grip. He'd been flirting with her on the boat because it had been fun and also because he'd wanted to see how he could manipulate her. In that situation, the power had all been on his side, and that's where he needed to keep it.

After leaving his house, he drove back to the gym, wanting to have a private word with Mick before Andrea could get to him. He half expected to see her pulling into the alley in front of him, but thankfully that didn't happen.

Mick was in his office now, going over some paperwork.

"Did you forget something?" Mick asked in surprise.

Alex walked in and shut the door behind him. "We need to talk."

"In a second." Mick punched out numbers on a calculator, adding up a string of invoices, and then swore.

"Problem?" Alex quizzed, dumping a pile of fitness magazines on the floor so he could take a seat in front of the desk.

"They raised the entry fee in the San Jose Boxing Competition in January."

"How much?"

"Three hundred and eighty-five dollars."

Alex rolled his eyes and dug into his pocket for his wallet.

"You want it in twenties or tens?"

"You shouldn't be walking around with that much cash." Mick motioned toward the wad in Alex's hand. "People like you get robbed down here."

"People like me know how to protect themselves. I have you to thank for that."

"Just don't get too comfortable, Alex. When you stop looking over your shoulder is when trouble comes. And I don't need any more money, so put that away. The check you gave me earlier will keep us going for quite a while.

"Good. But speaking of trouble, I need a favor."

"What's that?"

"I may have a problem."

Mick laughed, a knowing gleam in his eyes. "You definitely have a problem, and she's a beautiful blonde named Andrea."

"Yes, but she's not trouble in the way you mean. She's doing a story on me."

"That's not all she's doing on you."

He frowned at Mick's cheerful smile. "Look, Andrea wants to interview you. I probably shouldn't have brought her down here, but I can't take that back now."

"And you want me to cover for you." Mick leaned back in his chair and kicked his feet up on the desk. "I don't know if I should."

"Why not?"

"Secrets eat away at the soul."

"They also protect," he countered. "And you know I'm not just talking about myself."

"If you're so worried about your privacy, why did you agree to the interview?"

"Because I've never had a problem handling a reporter before."

Mick's grin broadened. "She got under your skin."

"Yeah," he admitted. "And she's determined to find out all my secrets."

"Did you really feel it was necessary to warn me to be quiet? I'm insulted, Alex. We've known each other a long time."

"Don't take it that way. Consider it a heads up."

"All right. Since this woman has you rattled, I'll do that. But I don't think it's just her story you're worried about. She's not like those flaky models you date. She's got brains and a mind of her own. And you've always liked a challenge."

Mick was right. He did like a challenge, and he definitely liked Andrea. Her sharp wit, her candor, and even her vulnerability had impressed him. And he had the strangest urge to try to impress her in return, which was really why he'd brought her to the gym in the first place. He'd wanted her to catch a glimpse of a man who did more than party with rich people. But that had been an impulsive mistake.

"I like a challenge," he said, realizing Mick was still waiting for him to comment. "But I'm not stupid. I won't jeopardize everything."

"What happens if she does find something out? What then?"

Alex's mouth tightened into a grim line at the thought. "I'd have to make sure she didn't use it."

"By doing what?"

"Whatever I have to."

"Maybe when Andrea gets here, I should offer her some boxing gloves. She might need them before you're through."

"All I need you to do is smile and tell her nothing. Hopefully, she'll get frustrated and give up."

Mick smiled. "And here I thought you'd forgotten how to be optimistic."

He reluctantly smiled back. "I thought I'd forgotten, too."

"When do you see her again?"

"Tonight. I'm taking her to a party. There will be lots of people around and no chance for private conversation." He paused, wondering why that didn't sound quite so appealing anymore. "At any rate, tonight should not be a problem."

* * *

Andrea was wrestling with a stubborn zipper on the back of her emerald green cocktail dress when the doorbell rang. Swearing under her breath, she gave the zipper another impatient tug, glaring at her expression in the mirror. The dress clung to her body like a second skin, and her blond hair tumbled around her shoulders in a mass of waves. She was actually a little amazed by her image. She looked downright sexy—like a party girl, a woman on a date, not a reporter on assignment. But she could hardly go to a cocktail party in her work clothes, and it was too late to change anyway.

The doorbell rang again, reminding her that there was no time for second thoughts. With one arm holding the back of her dress together, she stalked to the front door and threw it open, glaring at the man in the hallway.

"You're early," she said.

Alex raised one eyebrow and then consulted his Rolex watch. "Two minutes late, actually."

She let out a heavy sigh and stood back. "You might as well come in."

"Thank you. What's wrong?"

"My zipper is stuck."

"Let me help."

She reluctantly turned around, knowing he was going to catch a good view of her lacy bra and bare back.

"Nice," he murmured.

Her nerves tingled at the husky word.

"Just focus on the zipper."

"Not as easy as you might think," he said dryly. "You have a beautiful body, what I can see of it—"

"I'd rather you see less of it—so zipper, please."

She stared straight ahead, trying to concentrate on the long crack of plaster on the wall and not on Alex's warm fingers as they grazed her back. But the wall didn't do it for her, so she looked around the living room of her small apartment, suddenly aware of the overflowing laundry basket she'd set on the chair when she'd come up from the laundry room earlier, and the bridal magazines her sister had left on the coffee table, and the half-filled mug of coffee she'd drunk the night before while doing her research on Alex. She wasn't a complete slob, but her apartment was nowhere near as pristine clean as Alex's house. Then again, she didn't have a cleaning staff.

"This is really stuck," Alex said.

"Maybe I'll just wear something else."

"Give me a second. Don't give up so easily."

She normally didn't give up easily at all, but with Alex so close, her nerves were jumping, and she felt a reckless yearning take over her mind and body. She wanted to lean back against him, to feel his arms slide all the way around her waist. He would lower his head and his lips would touch the side of her neck, but he wouldn't stop there. He'd keep on kissing her. He'd pull the dress off her shoulders, and his mouth would drop to her breasts. He would call her beautiful and sexy in that deep, baritone voice. Then she would—

Stop! She would stop, she told herself, searching desperately for another distraction.

She turned her head to look at the opposite wall where her father's award-winning press clippings were framed and displayed. They reminded her of what was important. Her father's work had always been her inspiration. She had to stop acting like a woman around Alex and start acting like a reporter.

"I've got it." With a sigh of satisfaction, Alex pulled the zipper up the length of her back. "You're all set."

Andrea immediately stepped away from him, eager to get some breathing space. She fled into her bedroom, mumbling that she would be with him in a few minutes. When she got into the privacy of her room, she took several deep, calming breaths.

She was not going to be able to do her job if she let herself get turned on by the simple touch of his hand on her back. Walking to her dressing table, she picked up her brush and ran it briskly through her hair. Then she looked for some pins. She'd pull her hair into a knot, a business-like knot.

Her hand paused when a knock came at her door.

"Andrea? Don't put up your hair, okay?"

She didn't answer, caught between wanting to please him and wanting to feel more like a reporter than a date. She didn't usually let men dictate how she dressed or wore her hair, but there was something about his plea that got to her. So she gave in. They were going to a cocktail party, after all. Since she already had the dress on, she might as well go the rest of the way.

When she returned to the living room, Alex was standing in front of her bookshelves, examining the titles with open curiosity. He pulled out a thick volume that dissected World War II in fifty-six chapters. "Do you have insomnia? Because if so I can think of better ways to relax."

"It's a very interesting book."

"You've read all one-thousand pages?" he asked doubtfully.

"Actually I've never gotten past chapter four. The book belonged to my father. He was a history fanatic."

Alex waved his hand toward the bookshelf. "And the other military books?"

"All his. He loved spy stories. If he hadn't been such a good journalist, I think he might have joined the CIA. As it was, he was quite a legend in the news business. I'm not sure I can ever reach his level." Her voice cracked with emotion. "Sorry. I get a little carried away when I think about him. He died a long time ago. You'd think I'd be over it by now."

"Some things you never get over," Alex said, as a strong current of understanding flowed between them. "It looks like you're following in his footsteps. I'm sure he'd be proud."

"I hope so."

"Tell me about the rest of your family. Are you close to your mother?"

"We talk quite often, but we're very, very different. She does not get me, and I do not get her."

"What about your sister?"

"We're quite close. We're fraternal twins, and we're nothing alike, either, but there's a strong bond between us. I would do anything for her, and she would do anything for me." Andrea paused. "Laurel is getting married in a few weeks. I love her husband, and I'm super happy for her, but I do wonder sometimes how it will change our relationship."

"I guess that depends on how hard you work to keep your bond strong."

"I should probably work harder even now I tend to get obsessed with work and let everything else go. I'm Laurel's maid of honor, and I've been a huge slacker when it comes to the wedding plans. Thankfully, Laurel has a big wedding party so our other friends have been picking up the slack."

"I've never understood the big wedding party. Why does anyone need a dozen bridesmaids and groomsmen to get them down the aisle?"

"It's a celebratory send-off. And Laurel had to have seven bridesmaids because of a pact we made in college. I told you that we were part of a really tight group of friends. The day before we graduated we all went out together and swore that even if we drifted apart or ended up on opposite sides of the country, we would commit to coming back for each of our weddings, and we wouldn't let any excuses get in the way."

"That sounds—optimistic," Alex said with a dry smile.

She nodded. "Our promise didn't even make it two months. Jessica got married in a courthouse wedding with no bridesmaids because she found out she was pregnant. We were all really pissed off at her. But she also got divorced two years later, so after that we decided it was even more important that we keep our promise.

Laurel is the first to marry with all of us in the wedding, and I can't wait. Some of us live in the Bay Area, but it's been a long time since we were all together."

"You're lucky to have a close family and good friends."

"I am," she agreed. "And once again I am doing all the talking. We're going to have to switch that up sometime."

"Well, not right this second. We should get on the road."

"There's always a time issue when it's your turn to speak."

He shrugged. "We'll have to manage the clock a bit better."

"Oh, I think you're managing it quite well," she said dryly.

He gave her a smile. "There will be time for us to talk later."

"I hope you're right."

Chapter Six

While there was plenty of food at the party, there was absolutely no chance for them to speak privately. Andrea sipped her champagne and gazed around the crowded party, which was being held in a private dining room on the fiftieth floor of the Sterling Hotel. Floor to ceiling windows offered magnificent sweeping views of the city and the bay, and as with their dinner the previous night, the food was first class.

Alex was in the middle of a crowd of people, who seemed to hover intently on his every word. She knew it wasn't just his money and power that called them over, it was also his charisma. When he was in the room, everyone knew it. He was a magnet, and she could feel the pull from across the room. She had a feeling that even if he'd still been dirt poor, he would have been the center of attention.

She finished her champagne, set the glass down on an empty tray and moved towards him. It was about time she reminded Alex that she was there, too. When she reached the group surrounding him, she squeezed to the front of the circle, managing to dislodge a clingy redhead from his side.

She put a hand on Alex's arm and stood on tiptoe to whisper in his ear, "I'm back."

Alex didn't acknowledge the comment, but a small smile played across his lips. She moved a little farther forward, so she could see exactly who he was talking to. The crowd shifted at her movement, and suddenly she was face-to-face with a man she had hoped she would never see again, her ex-boyfriend, Douglas Wilmington.

She blinked in shock, hoping the horrible image would disappear, but Doug was gazing back at her with his perfect white teeth, his sky blue eyes, and his sun-streaked blond hair, and her stomach took a nosedive. She grabbed on to Alex's arm as if he were a buoy and she was about to drown.

"Andrea?" Doug said her name with surprise.

Of course he would be surprised to see her here. This kind of party was his world, not hers. "Hello, Doug," she managed to get out.

"You two know each other?" Alex asked.

Andrea nodded. "Yes."

"We were together for over a year," Doug added. "It's been a while though."

"Congratulations on your baby. Is your wife here?" she asked, even though it turned her stomach to make conversation with the man.

"No, she's at home with our child."

She didn't know what to say to that or what to say to him. Their relationship had ended badly. He'd been an asshole to her, and she'd been stupid enough not to see his bad traits a lot earlier in the relationship. But very few people would believe that Doug was anything but a great guy. Like Alex, he had a lot of charm.

"Maybe you and Wilmington can catch up later, Andrea," Alex said. "Why don't we get something to eat?"

"That sounds great."

"You're here with Alex?" Doug asked, more amazement in his voice.

Before she could answer, Alex said, "She is. I'm a lucky guy." Alex took her hand and led her across the room.

She blew out a grateful breath as she put some space between Doug and herself. "You know people are going to think I actually am your date," she said to Alex.

"You looked like you needed a save."

"Very perceptive. I did. Thank you."

"And I don't care if anyone thinks you're my date." He paused as they reached the end of the buffet line. "So you dated Doug Wilmington?"

She sighed. "I did—for far too long. It took me some time to realize that Doug liked my press connections more than he cared about me. As you may know, he's a lawyer who wants to be in politics. I was able to provide him with some good connections."

"I think he liked more about you than your connections."

She shrugged. "I don't know. Maybe. It doesn't matter. He used me, and not just for press; he also cheated on me."

"You're better off without him."

"I know that. He's the kind of man who looks good on paper, but in reality, not so much. My mother could never see that though. She really wanted us to get married. I disappointed her when we broke up."

"Did you tell her he cheated on you?"

"No," she admitted. "It was embarrassing. I don't know why I just told you."

"I'm a good listener."

He actually was a good listener, which she hadn't expected.

"Maybe you can't blame your mother for her opinion if you didn't tell her the truth," he added.

"My sister said the exact same thing, but my mother and I have a difficult relationship. She's very judgmental and critical, and I often fall short, so if I don't have to admit to a stupid mistake like picking a loser to date, I usually don't."

"But then you're protecting Doug and throwing yourself

under the bus. You're letting her blame you for the breakup. How does that improve your relationship?"

"It doesn't. But I can't seem to act more rationally around her. By the way, you're very good at analyzing people."

"I've always been interested in psychology."

"And you use that interest in your games, don't you?"

"It helps to know what drives people to do certain things, yes." He shifted his weight. "Do you want to get out of here and find some food elsewhere?"

"Absolutely."

"Do you like Thai?"

"I eat it at least once a week."

"There's a good takeout place down the street from here. It's a hole-in-the-wall, but you won't find better Thai food in the city."

"Lead the way."

* * *

Twenty minutes later, after picking up green curried chicken and Pad Thai, Alex drove Andrea toward the freeway leading out of the city.

"We're not going to your house?" she asked.

"I have a better idea. You keep saying you want to know more about me, so I'm going to take you to one of my favorite places."

"I like the sound of that."

"I thought you would. And, no, I'm not going to tell you where we're going until we get there."

"I wasn't even going to ask," she said dryly. "But I hope it's not too far, because the food smells delicious, and my mouth is watering."

"There's no traffic, so we should be there in about ten minutes."

She sat back in her seat to enjoy the ride, silently trying to guess where they might end up. But none of her guesses came close to their destination.

Alex turned off the freeway, driving down a frontage road that moved past the bay and the airport. Then he pulled onto a dirt strip facing the southernmost runway and shut off the engine. It was a dark and isolated spot, and it was definitely not somewhere she would have expected him to take her.

"I know we're at the airport, but why are we here?"

"You'll see," he said. There was just enough light coming from the adjacent runway to show the smile in his eyes. "Watch."

A moment later, a jumbo jet turned and sped down the runway in front of them, launching into the sky with a roar and a rumble that shook the car, and then there was nothing but silence.

"It never fails to impress me," Alex said quietly.

She glanced over at him. "So you like to fly, I guess."

"I do, but when I first started coming here, flying somewhere else seemed like an impossible dream."

His voice was quiet, reflective. She almost didn't want to ask another question, because he seemed lost in thought, and she was afraid any word from her would stop him from talking further. He'd put his guard back up and remember she was a reporter and someone who threatened his privacy.

He looked over at her. "No questions?"

"When did you find this place?"

"A long time ago."

"After your parents died?"

"Yeah," he said shortly. "We should eat. I hope you don't mind a picnic in the car?"

"If you don't mind food in this beautiful car, it's okay with me." She actually liked the idea of sharing a meal in complete and total privacy, no other people or distractions except the planes, of course. She pulled out the containers and a couple of plastic forks, and for a few minutes they ate in silence, the only break in the quiet coming from the jet engines.

"That was good," she said, sliding their empty containers into the bag. "I'll have to remember that place."

"I told you it was the best Thai food in town."

"You did. And you were not exaggerating." She paused as another plane took off. "How did you find this place?"

"For about six months, I lived a mile away—on the other side of the freeway. I used to come over here whenever I needed to get away."

"Who were you living with then?" she asked, trying to figure out what period of his life he was talking about.

"A foster family. There were a couple of different ones over a few years. This particular family had taken in four other kids, and it was a small house. It felt really crowded to me, so I got out whenever I could."

"Why did you end up going somewhere else?"

"I don't really remember."

She doubted that. Alex seemed like the kind of man who remembered everything.

"Let's get out of the car," he suggested.

"It's kind of cold," she protested.

"You can wear my coat."

"All right." She stepped out of the car and followed him over to the chain link fence.

He took off his coat and wrapped it around her shoulders. "How's that?"

"It's good."

Alex put his hands on the fence, linking his fingers around the wire as the next plane pulled into position. "This runway opened up the world for me. It made me feel like I could dream, like there was freedom somewhere, I just had to find a way to get to it."

"You certainly did that. You not only found a way to get on a plane, you found a way to own your own plane—didn't you?"

"I do have my own plane. I'll have to give you a ride some time."

"That would be amazing. I've never been on a private jet. Now you can go wherever you want. You're about as free as any man could be."

"I am." He shot her a quick look. "And I want you to know that I don't take my success and good fortune for granted, Andrea. I worked hard for it, probably a lot harder than anyone would believe."

"I don't doubt that. You faced a lot of challenges as a kid, but you didn't let those obstacles keep you down."

"I was too stubborn to give up. I knew there had to be more to life than the one I was living. There were people on these planes, people who'd found a way to take off on an adventure, maybe people like me." He paused. "One of my first games, Wing Rider, is based on all the days I spent standing on this fence."

She made a mental note to check out the game as soon as possible.

"It was my first bestseller," he added.

She liked that his childhood dream had turned into a reality. It seemed the best kind of justice. "Did you ever imagine you'd be this successful, this rich?"

"Yes," he said, looking her straight in the eye. "I've always believed that if you're going to dream, you should dream big. There are no barriers to the imagination, only in the real world. But you can move some of those barriers with persistence, determination and ambition."

"I really should be writing this down. Or do you mind if I tape our conversation with my phone?"

"I'd rather have you write what you remember from our

conversations, what sticks in your head as important. Everything else is worthless."

"But you just gave me a great, inspiring quote. You are someone to admire, Alex. I'll admit I didn't really know that when I first got this assignment, but I'm starting to really respect you and everything you've accomplished."

"I'm glad."

She looked through the fence as the engines of the jet in front of them began to roar. It seemed to move down the runway in slow motion, although she knew it had to be hitting speeds over a hundred miles an hour. The wheels lifted and the plane tilted, for a moment caught between earth and sky. It would either go up or come down. She caught her breath, lifting the plane with her mind. And then it was up and airborne, flying off for destinations unknown.

"It is incredible that man can move so quickly from one place to another," she said.

"Do you travel much, Andrea?"

"No, but I hope to do more in the future."

"Do you want to be a foreign correspondent like your father?"

She thought about his question. "For a while I did, but as I've gotten older, I've begun to realize that I don't want to live his career; I want to make my own way in the world. Although I haven't dreamt of having my own airplane or even a million dollars, I have imagined myself making a difference in the world in some way."

"I have no doubt that you will."

"If I can just get my interviewees to talk to me," she said with a sigh.

"I'm talking to you now, and I took you to the gym earlier. I also brought you here. You're way ahead of every other reporter I've talked to."

"I appreciate that. But I wasn't just referring to you."

"Are we back to the other secret story?"

"Yes. I thought I had a really good source, but he disappeared on me, and neither I nor my investigator have been able to find him."

"What do you think happened?"

"I believe he got scared. He was in a position to share some information about his company, something they were doing wrong, and I really believe he wanted to blow the whistle, but someone scared him off."

"Or paid him off," Alex suggested.

She frowned. "I did wonder about that. It's so frustrating. I feel like I let him slip through my fingers. I should have done a better job of cornering him, but I let him call the shots. I was playing it his way, and that didn't work."

"Does this person still work for the company?"

"No, the official word is that he resigned. I called his cell phone, but his number is no longer in service. I went by his apartment, and his neighbor said he'd left for an extended vacation. She wasn't sure where he'd gone. I worry that something bad happened to him because he was trying to talk to me."

"That's a leap."

"I don't want to believe it's true, but I have to consider all the options."

"You're not going to tell me what this story is about, are you?" Alex asked.

"I really can't. Sorry. I shouldn't have brought it up." She paused. "Getting back to you. Do you have a woman in your life?"

"No one serious."

"Have you been involved with anyone in the recent past? I know you've gone on a lot of dates, but has there been someone who stuck around awhile?"

"How long would you consider awhile?"

"Six months."

"Then no."

"Okay, what has been your longest relationship in the past five years?"

He thought for a moment. "Probably about two to three months."

"What happened?"

"The fire burned out."

She stared back at him. "On whose side?"

"Both sides. It was a mutual parting."

"So you're a serial dater?"

"That sounds bad. I don't think I want to be that," he said with a lighthearted grin.

"You're messing with me, aren't you?"

"I don't know what you mean."

"This is why you haven't had a relationship longer than three months. You don't take women seriously."

"And you seem to take things a little too seriously. It's a beautiful night. Relax, enjoy it. You don't have to work every second."

"I don't know how many seconds I'm going to have with you," she replied. "I don't want to waste them."

"If we're just going to talk about my love life, you are wasting them. I really have nothing momentous to share with you. And I don't date nearly as often as you think."

"Why not? You could have any woman you want."

"Could I have you?" he challenged.

She shivered at his words. "You don't want me. You just want to shake me up."

"I do want you, and I do want to shake you up," he said, taking a step in her direction.

She instinctive backed up, right into the fence. "Let's get back to the interview."

"What are you afraid of, Andrea?"

"I'm not afraid. I just want to get back to business."

"This is business. The business of you getting to know me." He put his hands on her waist. "I'm about to reveal something to you that I've never shown another reporter."

"What's that?" she asked breathlessly.

He lowered his head and his mouth covered hers.

She jumped at the heat of his lips, the sudden unexpected contact. She should have pushed him away, but instead she found herself sinking into the kiss, sliding her arms around his back, pressing her breasts against his chest. His mouth was warm and still spicy from the curry, and he kissed with same confidence and intensity that he seemed to bring to everything else in his life.

She kept telling herself she would end the kiss in a moment. She would move away. She would get back to the most important thing in her life, which was her job. But she didn't feel much like a reporter now. She felt like a woman—a woman filled with desire and need and an ache that started in her heart and ran through every muscle in her body.

Thankfully, the need to breathe finally broke them apart. She doubted she would have made a move otherwise.

Alex lifted his head and the steam of their heated breaths flowed around them. He stared into her eyes, and she wished for a few less shadows. If she could see him better, maybe she could read what he was thinking, but in the dim light, his expression was indecipherable.

She swallowed hard and drew in a breath. "That was…" The right word seemed impossible to find.

"Yeah," he said. "I completely agree."

"You agree it was unprofessional?" she asked, finally finding the word she was looking for.

"That's what you were going to say?" he asked with a frown.

No, she'd been searching for an adjective along the lines

of amazing, awesome, fantastic, unbelievable…but she wasn't going to tell him that. "I don't know. I don't want to talk about it. We should go." She slipped his coat off of her shoulders and handed it back to him. Then she headed to the car.

She was in her seat with the belt buckled a good minute or two before Alex finally slid behind the wheel. He started the engine, then looked over at her. "That was the best kiss I've had in a long time." His gaze lingered on hers for a long moment, then he shifted into drive and pulled out of the parking spot.

She looked out the window, his words rocketing around her head. Alex had said exactly what she'd been thinking, what she hadn't had the courage to say. What the hell were they going to do now?

Chapter Seven

Andrea still hadn't come up with an answer to that question when Alex walked her into her apartment building twenty minutes later. He'd insisted on leaving his car temporarily double-parked so that he could see her to her door, which seemed like a remarkably nice thing to do. Most of the guys she went out with were happy to pause the car while she jumped out, and they were usually gone before she entered her building.

On the other hand, Alex's insistence on accompanying her to her apartment created yet another awkward moment. Did she say goodnight at the door or invite him in?

She should invite him in so she could ask him more questions and get him back on the interview track. But inviting him into her apartment came with other problems, most notably the desire still ringing through her body after their kiss.

She slid her key into her lock and opened her door. "Do you want to continue our interview?"

"Not tonight."

She knew she should push, but she couldn't find the words. "Okay. What time should we meet tomorrow?"

"Actually, I'm going to have to pass on tomorrow."

"Why? I thought you'd cleared your weekend for this

interview."

"Something unexpected came up."

"When did that happen? And why didn't you mention it before now?"

"Because I don't have to clear my schedule with you," he said, a hard note in his voice.

She stared back at him. "Is this about what happened before?"

"No, it's not."

"Really? Because it seems like your sudden plans for tomorrow came out of nowhere."

"They didn't. I got a call earlier, before the cocktail party. I just didn't have a chance to mention the change in plans until now. Don't overthink this, Andrea. It was just a kiss."

"The best kiss you've had in a while," she couldn't help reminding him, feeling a little annoyed that he was suddenly blowing her off.

His lips curved into a smile. "I thought you didn't want to talk about it."

She didn't want to talk about it, and she was sorry she'd brought it up, because the memory only increased the tension between them. "I don't."

"Then I guess we'll touch base on Monday."

"Alex, we have so much to do. I only have ten days to write this piece, and I don't have much of anything to say yet."

"I don't think that's true. But if I have some time later tomorrow, I'll give you a call."

He paused, his gaze so dark and intense her stomach did a little flip-flop. Was he going to kiss her again?

The air between them sparked. She could practically see the fire, but when Alex moved, it wasn't to kiss her; it was to walk away.

Frustrated with him and with herself, she went into her apartment and shut the door, wondering how on earth she was going to write a serious story about a man she really just wanted to take to bed.

* * *

Alex drove back to his house, feeling extremely irritated with himself. The night had not gone at all as he'd planned, nor had any other part of the day. Andrea had gotten him off track in a big way. He'd not only taken her to the gym, he'd also shown her one of his private places where he went to think or escape. And he'd never taken anyone to the airport before, at least not that part of the airport. But he'd wanted to take her. He'd wanted to share something of himself, even if he couldn't share everything.

More importantly, he'd just wanted to be alone with her.

His plan to surround her with people and parties was bothering him as much as it was bothering her. Not because he wanted to tell her anything about himself, but because he wanted to know more about her. She was very different from the women he usually dated. She had a passion for her career, a true calling for what she did, and how many people could say that? She was honest and open and interested in everything, and he liked that she didn't choose her words too carefully, that she spoke from the heart.

But while all those qualities made him like her more, it also made it more difficult for him to keep her at arm's length, to stay professional.

She was right—that kiss had not been professional, and while he tried to tell himself that kissing her was just part of the plan to keep her distracted from asking questions, he knew deep down that he'd just wanted to taste her lips, feel her mouth under his. And he hadn't wanted to stop with a kiss. It had taken all of his willpower to leave her at her door.

But he wasn't completely stupid. He couldn't let desire

take over his good sense. Andrea might be one of the most interesting and beautiful women he'd met in a long time, but she was also a reporter. And when she went after a story, she went all in.

He needed to step back and regroup. Hopefully, twenty-four hours without seeing her would send his blood flowing in the right direction again—back to his brain.

* * *

With Alex off her Sunday schedule, Andrea joined her friends and fellow bridesmaids for Sunday brunch at the Bella Mar Café, a seafood restaurant famous for its Sunday brunch and spectacular views of the San Francisco Bay. She was excited to get together with at least some of the girls and hopefully talk about Laurel's bachelorette party. She knew her sister would not be making it to brunch, as Laurel's fiancé's father was having a birthday party today.

After parking her car in the garage across the street, she ran into her friend Liz Palmer, and they exchanged a happy hug then walked to the elevator together. Liz was a pretty dark blonde with big brown eyes that were always sharp and inquisitive. In their group, Liz had been the smart, somewhat serious one, the girl who generally didn't make as many impulsive mistakes as the rest of them. And Andrea had always considered Liz's advice to be spot-on.

"How did the hunt for the wedding photographer go?" Andrea asked, remembering that Laurel, Liz and Kate had spent Saturday in search of a replacement.

"Great," Liz replied. "Laurel liked the second guy we spoke to. We showed his portfolio to your mom, and she signed off. So crisis averted."

"Thank goodness. Now tell me how your dad is doing."

Shadows entered Liz's eyes. "Not well. He's had cancer

for a while, as you know. They've been trying to put it in remission, but nothing has been working."

"I'm really sorry."

"I know. It's rough, but he's a strong man, and he's a fighter. We're hoping things will turn around."

"How is it at work without him there?"

"Not great. Dad's partners are acting like he's already gone, and I'm a reminder that he's not. They can't just ride over his ideas or his part of the partnership while I'm there. Anyway, we don't need to talk about all that. I'm thrilled to see you here. I wasn't sure you were going to make brunch today," she added as they got on the elevator and rode it down to the street level.

"I wasn't either, but my schedule opened up."

"Kate thought you might be tied up with some sexy millionaire you're interviewing," she said with a curious smile.

"He wasn't available to talk to me today."

"But you've been spending some time with him, so what's he like?"

"He's really attractive, charming, has a great smile and sense of humor. He doesn't seem to take himself too seriously. But he's also got some mystery to him. There are shadows in his eyes. He's hard to read. I feel like I've gotten to know him a little, but there's so much more to find out."

"You like him, don't you?"

She frowned. "How I feel about him isn't relevant to the article I'm writing."

"I don't care about the article; I care about you," Liz said. "And it's been awhile since you liked someone—Doug really did a number on you."

That was certainly true. "Well, I don't want to like Alex. He's business. And that's all he's going to be."

Thankfully, she didn't have to say more since they'd arrived at the restaurant. They immediately saw their friends sitting at a large corner table by the window.

Kate, a beautiful, blue-eyed brunette, was the first to see them and gave a welcoming wave. Next to Kate was Julie, a cool, quiet blonde, who worked as a fundraiser for a children's charity. Then there was Maggie, a gorgeous redhead with sparkling green eyes. Maggie worked as a front desk clerk at the luxurious Stratton Hotel in the Napa Valley, but today she'd made the trip from the wine country to San Francisco. Finally, there was Elisa, a striking Hispanic woman with dark brown hair, matching eyes and an incredibly beautiful smile that always lit up her eyes. Elisa worked at a dance studio and had always been the most musical and passionate member of their group of friends. The only one missing was Jessica, who had recently moved to San Diego with her five-year-old son to take a new teaching job. But Jessica had promised to be there for the wedding and hopefully a few other bridal events.

"Am I dreaming?" Kate asked in amazement as they took their seats. "Are you really here, Andrea?"

"We were beginning to think you found a new group of friends," Maggie put in.

"I've been busy with work," she said.

"As always," Julie said with a knowing smile. "We all work, you know," she added pointedly, but there was a smile at the end of her words. "However, we're very glad you could make it."

"It makes my long drive from Napa even more worthwhile," Maggie added. "It's been too long, Andrea. Is Laurel coming, too?"

"No, she has to do something with her soon-to-be in-laws," she replied. "Which is fine, because I want to talk about the bachelorette party today. I know I haven't been the greatest maid-of-honor so far, but that changes now."

"You still have time to get it right," Kate said.

"I hope so." She paused as the waiter set down a mimosa

in front of her. "I like the service."

"We went ahead and ordered drinks and appetizers," Elisa said.

"Great. I'm starving."

"So Kate told us about your new assignment, and we're all dying to know what Alexander Donovan is like," Maggie said. "Is he as hot as his pictures?"

"Yes."

"And…" Kate prodded.

"You'll have to wait and read my article," she said, knowing there was no way they were going to let her get away with that. She sipped her drink as they fired questions at her.

"Is he as rich as they say?"

"What does his house look like?"

"Who is he sleeping with?"

"When are you seeing him again?"

She smiled, waiting for them to run out of steam. When they were together, it was always like this. They could jump from topic to topic, sometimes finishing each other's thoughts without missing a beat. Even though it had been years since they'd shared a common bathroom in the college dorms, and even though they didn't see each other as often as they liked, when they got together it was as if they'd only been apart for a second.

"Are you guys done?" she asked.

"Only if you start talking," Liz said.

"Alex Donovan is a rich, attractive, sexy man with a huge business, many friends and a lot of power. That's why he was picked to be the magazine's *Man of the Year*. He came from nothing and he has made millions or billions, I'm not even sure how much he's worth. I think his story will inspire a lot of people. But I'm still trying to get to the real man, which might take some time."

"Sounds like that would be a fun time," Maggie said with

a grin.

"He is charming."

"Do you think he's interested in you?" Kate asked.

"No. I'm way too serious for him. He likes party girls."

"But he is single, right?" Kate pressed.

"He appears to be, but there are dozens of women around him all the time."

"You can handle the competition," Julie said. "You've always liked a challenge."

"I like my job more, and right now my focus is on writing a good story. Unfortunately, Alex seems better at getting me to talk than I am at getting him to open up."

"How do you mean?" Julie asked.

"Well, last night at a party that Alex took me to, we ran into Doug."

There was a collective groan from her girlfriends, all of whom at one point or another had heard her sad story and either cried with her, hugged her, or shared gallons of ice cream with her.

"How did that go?" Maggie asked with compassion. Maggie was the nurturer in the group, the one who usually mothered them when they were down.

"It was thankfully brief. Doug made some snarky comment, but I think he was a little taken aback to see me with Alex. I didn't bother to explain just what I was doing with him."

"Good," Liz said approvingly. "That man treated you horribly. He should know that he made a huge mistake."

"I doubt he cares. He's married and has a baby now. It's weird how fast things can change. Anyway, enough about me; I want to hear about all of you." She turned to Kate first. "Is my mother driving you to a nervous breakdown?"

"She's not that bad. She knows what she wants, of course, but so far I've managed to keep her happy."

"You'll have to tell me that secret sometime. Okay, on to the bachelorette party. Does anyone have any ideas?"

"I do," Kate said tentatively. "I thought we could do a spa day at the Stratton next Saturday. Maggie said she could get us some rooms at a discount."

"As well as reservations at the most exclusive restaurant in Napa," Maggie put in.

"But only if you want to do that, Andrea," Kate said. "I don't want to overstep."

Andrea looked around at her friends and realized that they were picking up the slack for her again. "It sounds perfect. Laurel loves going to the spa, so I know she'll enjoy the trip."

"We can mix in some wine tasting," Elisa added. "My friend works at a winery and could get us a private tasting if we want."

"Sold. You are all amazing."

Kate nodded. "Does next weekend work for you?"

"I'll make it work," she promised.

"Great. Let's put it on the calendar then. Don't anyone make a date for that night," Kate ordered.

"I'll try to keep my schedule free," Liz said dryly. "But you know I'm really in demand on Tinder these days."

Andrea laughed. "You are not doing that dating site again. I thought you got off of it after the last loser made you pay for dinner and a very expensive cab ride."

"I was bored," Liz said. "I had a weak moment. I'm getting off today."

"Have you met anyone interesting?" Julie asked.

"No. I don't know where the interesting men are, but they certainly aren't on there."

"I think Andrea has found the most interesting man in San Francisco," Kate said.

"Yeah, if you don't want him, maybe you should throw him our way," Julie said with a laugh.

"Sorry, girls, Alex is all mine—at least until the story is done."

Andrea settled back in her seat and sipped her mimosa as the conversation changed to Maggie's latest adventure at the front desk of the Stratton. As she listened to her friends talk about their lives, she felt happy for the first time in a long while. She needed these women, these moments of grounding with people who knew her better than anyone else. She was going to do better at getting together in the future. No more missed brunches or lunches. These were her girlfriends, and she needed to stay close.

As she thought about all the secrets they had shared over the years, her mind turned back to Alex. There had to be someone who knew Alex's secrets, too.

Chapter Eight

Andrea found Mick in the gym Sunday afternoon. She waited while he ran a couple of kids through a boxing lesson, appreciating his quiet, firm patience. The man commanded respect, and the more she studied him, the more certain she became that this visit was going to be a waste of time. Still, she had to try. Even a small detail might help her flesh out her article on Alex.

Mick walked over to her with a smile on his face. "Back so soon?"

"I have a question or two for you about Alex. Do you have a few moments?"

"I can make some time. Come on back to the office."

She followed him down a hall and into a small, cluttered space. He grabbed a pile of t-shirts off of a chair and waved her toward the seat. Then he sat down behind the desk.

"Now, what can I do for you?" he asked.

"You know I'm writing an article on Alex's life. He mentioned to me that you let him sleep on the couch here in this office." She glanced at the small couch that was no bigger than a loveseat and couldn't imagine it had been very comfortable. But at least Alex had had a warm, dry place to sleep. It was still hard to really understand the life Alex had led as a kid and the one he led now.

"He needed a place to stay until he could graduate from high school."

"He said you really wanted him to stay in school."

"I did. I dropped out when I was fifteen. Regretted it for a very long time. I didn't want Alex to do the same."

"What was he like back then?"

Mick thought for a moment. "He had a lot of anger in him, but he was able to direct it in a positive way. He was a stubborn, determined kid. I knew he'd make something big out of his life, and he certainly did that."

"Yes," she agreed. "Alex seems to know a lot of people, but what he doesn't appear to have are really close friends or long-term friends."

"Well, he moved around as a kid, and once you get rich, it's hard to have real friends—at least that's what they tell me," Mick said with a self-deprecating grin.

"Me, too," she said with a smile.

"Is there anything you can tell me about Alex that maybe only you and a handful of people know?"

"Sure, I could tell you something."

She could see by the sparkle in his eyes that because he could didn't mean he would. "But you're not going to."

"Alex is a good friend of mine. I don't talk about him. He doesn't talk about me."

"He's not just a friend, he's also an investor in the gym, isn't he?"

"He helps out, probably more than he should. But Alex is the kind of man who gives back when he can." Mick paused. "I will tell you this about Alex. When he cares about someone, he goes all in. He's intensely loyal and incredibly generous, and not just with me."

"What about his faults? He must have a few."

"He's definitely not perfect."

"Would you care to share any small detail?"

"You're as stubborn as he is. The two of you are going to butt heads."

"We're already doing that," she admitted. "I don't really understand why. I want to write a good story about him, but he wants to keep me at arm's length."

"Somehow, I don't think he wants to keep you that far away," Mick said, a speculative gleam in his eyes. "But he probably should."

She shifted a little uncomfortably under his gaze. "Why?"

"Because if he doesn't keep his guard up, you'll have him on the ropes."

"Is that a boxing metaphor?"

"I suppose it is," he said with a grin. "But then life is a battle, isn't it? You have to learn to roll with the punches."

She smiled back at him. "You have a bunch of those, don't you?"

"I could go on all day, but I won't. I have a class starting in a few minutes."

"Well, I appreciate your time. If I have more questions, can I speak to you again?"

"Why don't you come back Wednesday night? I'm starting a new self-defense class for women. We're trying to make the gym a little less testosterone heavy."

"If I take the class, will you tell me more about Alex?"

"Tell you what, I'll answer one question for each woman you bring."

"Really? And that wouldn't be disloyal to Alex?"

"Well, I can't promise you'll like all my answers, but I'll do my best to give you a little more insight."

She stood up. "Okay, you've got yourself a deal, Mick."

"Good. I'll see you Wednesday."

She turned toward the door, then glanced back at him. "Are you going to tell Alex about our agreement?"

"I'll let you do that."

"He won't like it."

"Well, that's his problem, isn't it?"

"I guess it is."

* * *

Andrea spent the rest of Sunday writing up what she knew about Alex so far and then searching the Internet for more details. Unfortunately, every news report on Alex was the same. He'd told a similar story to every reporter in every single interview. She supposed she should feel a little special that at least he'd taken her to meet Mick and see the gym and had also shared his love of airplanes and airports with her, but she still needed more.

After a restless night of sleep, she went into her office on Monday with a new plan. As soon as she got to her desk, she put in a call to the magazine's private investigator. Joe was not only an ex-cop, he had excellent cyber skills, and he could usually get information no one else could find, although even he had come up short in trying to locate her source on the car seat story.

"Andrea, I told you I'd call you if I came up with anything," Joe said shortly.

"I'm not calling about that. But I don't understand how a man could disappear off the face of the earth."

"I admit I'm stumped," Joe said. "But I haven't given up."

"Good."

"So what do you need today?"

"Information on another interview subject—Alexander Donovan. He's our cover for the *Man of the Year* issue."

"Donovan is a fairly public figure. Do you think there's something he's hiding?"

"That's what I want you to find out." There were often shadows behind Alex's smile, and she really wanted to know where they came from. "I need the information as soon as possible."

"Of course you do. I'll get back to you."

"Thanks." She hung up the phone, having the strangest feeling that she'd just started something in motion she might regret.

* * *

By Tuesday, Alex knew that he couldn't put off speaking to Andrea any longer, so he finally returned one of her calls and suggested a tour of the company for three o'clock that afternoon. He wanted to keep the interview in a business environment so there would be fewer temptations. Here in his offices, he was in charge. This was his turf, and there wouldn't be any surprises.

Still, as he waited for her to arrive he paced in front of his window, feeling restless and impatient. He told himself the sooner she got there, the sooner he could get rid of her. But the truth was that he just wanted to see her again.

He'd been dreaming about her blue eyes, her sweet, sexy mouth, the tiny freckle at the corner of her nose, and her silky smooth blonde hair. He drew in a breath, feeling even more worked up about her.

What a mess he'd gotten himself into. He never should have agreed to do the story. He never should have suggested a reporter follow him around. Most importantly, he never should have kissed Andrea, because now all he could think about was doing it again. And he'd been thinking about it at very inopportune times, like when he was in the middle of business meeting when his focus should have been on the company's profit and loss statement and not on Andrea.

He needed to finish things off. End the interview and never see her again. Nothing could happen between them. She would always be a reporter, and he would always have secrets.

A knock came at his door, followed by Ellen's voice. He turned away from the window as Ellen ushered Andrea into the office.

His heart jumped against his chest at the sight of her. She was even prettier than he remembered. She wore a dress today, a figure-hugging dark blue dress that clung to her breasts and hips. A pair of three-inch heels showed off her legs. They made her seem taller and even more determined. He was going to have his hands full with her. That thought was both really enjoyable and somewhat disturbing.

"Alex," she said, a wary note in her voice. "Thanks for finally returning my call."

"I apologize for the delay. I had some unexpected business come up."

"So you said on Saturday. Is everything all right?"

"It's all good. Are you ready for the tour?"

"Absolutely. I'd love to see where the magic happens," she said with a smile.

"I'm afraid I won't be able to show you too much magic. Our engineering and software development departments are off limits. We have to protect our proprietary information."

"Then what are you going to show me?"

"We'll start with what I call the think tank. Follow me." He led her out of the executive offices and down a long hallway. At the end of the corridor were two glass doors that opened into a luxurious lounge.

"This is nice," Andrea murmured.

He nodded, glancing around the room. There were massage chairs in front of the bay windows, comfortable couches in cozy seating areas, a pool table in one corner and on the far side of the room was a gaming area. There were at least a dozen monitors, game players and computers. Next to the video equipment were pinball machines and an air-hockey table.

"That looks like an arcade," she murmured. "Do you come here to relive your past life where you worked at the miniature golf course arcade?"

"No, I created the area to inspire my workers. I want them to play everything from the lowest tech to the highest tech game. I want them to get creative, let their imaginations soar. I want them to help me create games that no one else has ever envisioned."

She nodded. "That makes sense."

"My employees work long hours, so I try to make their time at work as comfortable as possible. In addition to this lounge, we have a gourmet cafeteria upstairs and a quiet zone where people can stretch out for a nap. We also offer a car service, a laundry pickup, and we bring in physical therapists and visiting nurses to deliver therapy sessions, flu shots and wellness seminars."

"You've thought of everything."

"I take care of the people who work for me."

"I can see that. If I'd known how much fun tech companies were when I was in college, I might have changed my major."

"I seriously doubt that, not when you were reporting in the fifth grade."

"True. I have wanted to be a reporter forever, but the lounge at *World News Today* consists of a vending machine, a table and a coffeemaker."

Despite her words, he could see the pride in her eyes. She loved her job and she wasn't motivated by money but by passion. He liked that. He understood that. Because even though he'd made more money in the last five years than he'd ever imagined making in his entire lifetime, he still worked because he loved his business.

"What's that?" Andrea asked as she pointed to a spiral

staircase that seemed to end at he ceiling. "The stairway to nowhere?"

He grinned. "We call it the stairway to the stars." He led her across the room, pushed a button, and the ceiling over the staircase opened up.

She followed him up the stairs to the roof. As she stepped out, she said, "Oh, my God, this is amazing. What a view."

"It's what sold me on this building."

She walked around the deck, pausing here and there to take in a new part of San Francisco, finally ending up by two large telescopes. "Who uses these?"

"Anyone who wants to. Despite the city lights, you can do some serious stargazing with those telescopes. You'll have to come back at night." As soon as he said the words, he regretted them. His goal was to finish this interview off today or tomorrow and not extend future invitations to Andrea.

"That would be interesting," she said. "I studied a little astronomy in college, but I don't remember much." Pausing, she tilted her head, giving him the thoughtful look he was coming to expect.

Andrea was always trying to figure him out. And while at times he appreciated her desire to really get to know the man behind the games, her scrutiny always put him on edge. He wasn't used to anyone trying to get past his barriers. Since he'd gotten rich and famous, he'd acquired more walls between himself and others, and fewer people tried to breach his defenses. But Andrea was doing everything she could to slip past his guard, and he needed to keep his wits about him. That would be a lot easier if he didn't like her so much.

"What?" he asked when her stare went on far too long.

"Just thinking about how you like trains, planes and games and now telescopes. You're always thinking about ways to escape, to soar, to get your feet off the ground."

"Very perceptive. Is that going in your article?"

"We'll see. Do you think you would have been so focused on looking up and outward if you hadn't lost your parents, hadn't ended up having to fend for yourself at a time when most kids are coddled and protected?"

He shrugged. "Who's to say? I don't like to play the 'what if' game. It doesn't get me anywhere."

"I thought you liked to play every game," she teased.

He tipped his head. "Good point. But while my past is part of who I am, I think what drives me comes from the inside. You and I are not very different, Andrea. You have as much ambition as I do."

"Maybe, but I obviously haven't been as good at turning my ambition into profit or fame."

"Well, I have a few years on you. I have no doubt that you're fully capable of getting everything you want."

"I hope so. But again we're starting to talk about me, and this interview is about you," she reminded him.

"You're more interesting. What did you do this weekend?"

She hesitated. "I had brunch with my friends."

"The bridesmaids?"

"Yes, we planned my sister's bachelorette party."

"Where are you going—Vegas?"

"No, Vegas is not Laurel's style. We're going to do a spa retreat in Napa. One of my friends, Maggie, works at a fancy hotel up there. She's setting it all up."

"Sounds nice. What else did you do?"

She stared back at him. "You talked to Mick, didn't you?"

"Apparently, so did you." He hadn't been surprised to hear from Mick about Andrea's visit, and while Mick had assured him that no dark secrets had slipped past his lips, he couldn't help wondering what Andrea had gotten out of their conversation.

"Mick has a lot of respect for you, and he's a loyal friend.

But you already knew that, Alex."

"I did."

She stared back at him, more puzzlement in her eyes. "Who is your best friend, Alex?"

"Best friends are for girls and little kids."

"Oh, come on, that's not true. You're splitting hairs. If you don't like the word 'best', then tell me who your good friends are."

"You've met a bunch of them already."

She shook her head. "I mean people like Mick, people who really know you. What about kids you grew up with, went to high school with—do you keep in touch with any of them?"

"No," he said shortly. "My friends are the people you've met as well as some coworkers you haven't met."

"When do I get to meet them?"

"Andrea, you're not writing an encyclopedia. You don't need to interview everyone I've ever talked to in my life. How long is this article?"

"It's long enough to warrant as much information as I can gather," she retorted. "And I don't tell you how to make games, so don't tell me how to do my job."

Anger sparkled in her blue eyes, which only made them prettier. "I wasn't telling you how to do your job, but I think you're trying to make something out of nothing. You know my past. You know what I do now. What more do you want?"

"A lot more," she snapped. "You haven't told me anything about your parents."

"I don't talk about them."

"Exactly. And I know only basic facts about what happened in your teens. Your early twenties are still a mystery to me. There seem to be big gaps between working in a video arcade and running a billion-dollar company. I don't know who you talk to when you're down or whether you've ever really been in love with anyone. I don't know what you want to do tomorrow or next year or ten years from now."

"Neither do I. I don't have my life planned out. I stopped making plans a long time ago. I live in the moment."

"That's not true. You plan game releases a year out at least."

"Fine, I make business plans, but not personal ones."

"Why not?"

"Because I don't." He strode forward, stopping just inches away from her.

"You're afraid," she said.

"You're calling me a coward?" he asked in astonishment. "I've been called a lot of things, but not that."

"You're afraid to want something in case you don't get it. In business, it doesn't matter. But in your personal life, it does. You lost a lot as a kid, your parents, your aunt, your whole world was shattered. So now you don't have close friends. You don't count on people. You don't expect anything, because then you won't be disappointed."

"You think you have me figured out," he murmured. She actually wasn't that far off base. Not all of her assumptions were true, but some of them were. He shouldn't have been surprised. She was a smart woman with an analytical mind, but it wasn't her mind he was interested in right now.

"I think I've figured a few things out," she amended, wariness flashing in her eyes as he slid his arms around her. "Alex?"

"You're right about some things. I don't count on anyone but myself. And perhaps I don't make plans because when I used to do that, I was almost always slapped down. But I'm not as closed-off as you think. I have friends. I've had women in my life. And I'm not afraid of life. I'm ready for the next curve to get thrown. In fact, I'm not waiting for it to come to me; I'm going after it. I'm going after it right now."

She stiffened, desire in her eyes, as he made his intent extremely clear.

"Do you really think this is a good idea?

"Probably not. But I've been thinking about kissing you since the last time, and if you don't want this to happen, you better tell me now."

"It's hard to fight you and myself," she said with a soft sigh.

"Then don't."

The heat that had been simmering between them sparked and flamed with the touch of their lips. He took the kiss deeper, wanting to take her mouth, her body, every part of her that she wanted to give.

He hauled her up against his chest, needing to feel her soft curves, needing to be as close to her as he could get.

Andrea came willingly, putting her arms around his neck as her tongue tangled with his. God, she tasted good—a hint of paradise, a little bit of heaven, a soft place to fall. He'd never wanted to fall before. He'd always wanted to be in control. But right now he was on shaky ground, and he didn't give a damn.

Kissing her wasn't enough, but just like the last time they were nowhere near a bed or a couch or even a little more privacy.

He lifted his head. Andrea stared back at him, her lips swollen from passion, her eyes bright and dazed and a little needy.

"What is wrong with me?" she murmured, as she tucked her hair behind her ear. "You make me forget where I am, what I'm doing."

"You do the same to me."

"We have to find a way to finish this interview and be done with each other."

He stared back at her. He wanted to be done with the news article but not with her. "Can you have someone else at the magazine write the article?"

She immediately shook her head. "No, I can't. I need this story. I told you I wasted the magazine's time and money the last six weeks. I have to do a good job on this assignment. I know you can understand that."

He understood she was putting her job first. He shouldn't care or even judge, because he usually did the same thing when it came to business, but it didn't bother him. "Fine," he said shortly. "Let's go back to my office."

She put a hand on his arm, "Alex, wait."

"What?"

She stared back at him. "I like you."

His muscles tightened at her words.

"And as crazy as this may sound, I actually missed you," she added.

That didn't sound crazy at all. He'd missed her, too.

"I've never been in this position before," she continued. "I've never had this kind of crazy attraction to someone I'm supposed to be writing about, so I'm probably not handling this very well. And maybe I should give the story to someone else, but I really don't want to, so can we find a way to work together?"

How could he say no to the plea in her eyes? And it wasn't just the plea, it was her honesty that undid him. He hadn't known too many people who told the truth with such charm and vulnerability. She was putting herself out there, and he wasn't going to be the one to hurt her. "Okay," he said. "We'll get back to business."

Relief flooded her expression. "Good."

They walked back to his office in silence. But when they reached Ellen's desk, she stopped them.

"There you are," Ellen said. "I was just about to come looking for you, Alex. Did you forget that you have to be at the dentist in twenty minutes?"

He frowned. "That's not today. It can't be six months yet."

"It's been over a year and a half," Ellen said pointedly. "You cancelled the last two appointments. And don't even try to tell me to cancel now. You're going. I know you hate the dental chair, but you have to take care of your teeth."

Maybe it was just as well he had an appointment. A little time and space from Andrea would probably help put them back on the right track. He sent Andrea an apologetic look. "Sorry, but I have to go."

"Can we meet later?"

"I have a dinner meeting with some potential investors."

"Tomorrow then?"

"I'll give you a call when I know my schedule." Alex took his car keys from his assistant and headed out.

"Any chance you could help me set up an appointment with him?" Andrea asked Ellen.

"I would love to, but Alex said he wanted to handle your interviews personally."

"How long have you worked for Alex?" she asked.

"Nine years."

"What kind of an employer is he?"

"Fair, honest and hardworking. He treats me with respect. I have no complaints." Her tone offered no shades of gray.

Andrea smiled, trying to ease the tension on the older woman's face. "It's clear from your tone that you're very loyal, and Alex must have done something right to inspire that loyalty. I just wish I could get a clearer picture of who he is away from work."

"You'll have to ask him."

"He hasn't been very forthcoming."

"Well, he has a reason to be protective. Everyone wants a piece of him now. It's difficult for him to know who to trust. Some people just want to use him to get ahead."

There was a warning note in Ellen's voice now. Andrea

was not going to get anything from Alex's assistant.

"Just for the record," Andrea said. "Alex wasn't forced to do this interview, and I've been completely up front with him. I have a job to do, and I'm going to do it. "

"Then you shouldn't pretend to be his friend," Ellen said sharply.

She sucked in a quick breath at the harsh words. "I'm not pretending," she protested. "And I wouldn't even say we're friends." Actually, she didn't know what they were to each other.

"I saw your lipstick on his face, Ms. Blain."

There was no way she could explain that away.

"I told Alex not to do this interview," Ellen continued. "And I don't trust you for a second. I've never met a reporter who wasn't after a juicy secret. You want to dig into Alex's life, and you won't care at all what harm you do."

"Is there a juicy secret?"

"Your question just proves my point." Ellen shook her head. "If you'll excuse me, I have work to do." The woman turned her gaze back to her computer.

Andrea had no choice but to leave. As she walked back to her car, she couldn't get Ellen's words about a secret out of her head. The woman had not meant to intrigue her with anything; she'd been trying to push her away. But there was something in Ellen's gaze that Andrea couldn't quite shake.

Alex had a secret. A secret Ellen didn't want her to find. What the hell was it?

Chapter Nine

Andrea was still ruminating about what Alex could possibly be hiding when she got up Wednesday morning. She took a long, hot shower to get the knots out of her neck and shoulders. It had been another restless night. She certainly hadn't gotten much sleep since she'd met Alex.

She'd just finished drying her hair when her phone rang.

"What are you doing right now?" Alex asked.

Her heart skipped a beat at the sound of his voice. "Uh, waking up."

"I know just the thing to help that."

She was almost afraid to ask. "What's that?"

"A run. I'm just about to go for my morning run. If you want to talk, come with me."

"You want me to interview you while we're running?" she asked in dismay.

"It's the only time I have today. Afraid you can't keep up with me, Andrea?"

Never one to let a challenge pass by, she said, "Of course I can keep up with you. Where do you want to meet?"

"The Marina Green. I'll show you one of my favorite runs."

"Awesome," she replied as she ended the call.

She really wished she'd kept up her gym workouts the

past few months. If there was ever a time she needed to keep up on a run, it was probably today.

* * *

"What do you think? Do you want to go another mile?" Alex slowed his run down to a jog as they neared the base of the majestic Golden Gate Bridge. He looked over at Andrea with amusement in his eyes. "Or are you tired?"

She had a pain in her side, but she couldn't tell him that because she was still trying to catch her breath from the two miles they'd just run.

"We'll take a break," he said decisively, slowing down to a walk.

She nodded, relieved by that decision. She walked with him another fifty yards then came to a stop by a low cement wall that ran along the bay.

"Okay?" Alex asked, coming up next to her.

"I'm fine," she finally got out. "How often do you run?"

"Four or five times a week. You?"

"Almost never. But I do the elliptical at the gym when I have time."

"Which is how often?"

"Almost never."

He grinned. "You should have told me."

"I wanted the time to interview you."

"And you hate to admit weakness. It's just like when you didn't tell me you get seasick."

She made a face at him. "You don't have to worry. I'm not going to throw up today."

"Thank God for that. So what do you want to ask me?"

"Many things."

"Let's start with one."

She thought for a moment and then asked the question

that had been rolling around in her head all night. "Is there something in your past that you don't want me to know?"

He didn't flinch at her words, but the light left his eyes as he stared back at her. "Why would you ask me that?"

"Just wondering why you're trying to keep me at a distance. I figure there must be a reason why you're so cagey."

"I like my privacy. I don't think anyone in the world would enjoy someone poking their nose into every corner of their life. I doubt you would."

"If I agreed to an interview, I'd expect that."

He waved his hand in the air. "Next question."

"Fine. We'll move on. You push yourself hard in business. I was looking through your company brochure, the list of new releases planned for the coming year. You're moving at a very rapid pace."

"That's the gaming world."

"But you have done so much already. When will it be enough? When will you slow down?"

"I don't know that it will ever be enough, or that I'll ever slow down. I like what I do. My games are not just entertaining; they're educational. And kids need to be able to learn and have fun at the same time."

"So it's truly the games that drive you and not the money?"

"Yes. I can't deny that I enjoy having money now. Not having had it for a lot of years has made me appreciate my good fortune. I don't take it for granted, and I do try to share."

"Which brings us to philanthropy. I've been researching your long list of charity donations. You do spread the wealth around."

"I try."

"I noticed that you've been part of Big Brothers and have been supporting women and family shelters here in the city. Did your experience with foster care lead you in that direction?"

"Absolutely."

"I also read that you're starting a foundation to oversee your philanthropic efforts. Will that foundation be exploring other areas in which you might want to invest?"

"That's their mission. What else?"

She sighed, knowing that she just wasn't asking the right questions, but she couldn't think of how to get him to crack, other than to kiss him. That was the only thing that seemed to loosen him up. But she'd already told herself that wasn't going to happen again.

"Are we done?" Alex asked.

"Not quite. I asked you before about a girlfriend and you said you hadn't been seriously involved with anyone in a few years, but I wonder if you have ever been in love?"

He hesitated. "I don't know about love, but when I was in my early twenties, things got serious with one woman."

"Really?" she asked, surprised that he finally hadn't dodged a question or given her a one-word answer. "Who was it?"

He hesitated as a trio of women came down the trail. After they passed by, he said, "Her name was Valerie. We were together almost a year, but we were young. I was twenty-one and had little to no money at that point. I was scraping by, working a bunch of jobs. She was also twenty-one and eager to live the good life, so eventually she left me for a better prospect. Looking back, it was a good thing. She hated to fly, and she thought video games were stupid."

Andrea saw the hint of pain in his eyes. "You're making light of what must have hurt. No one likes to be used or pushed aside for a better prospect."

"Honestly, she hurt my pride more than anything else. I hated the fact that I had misread her so badly. I thought I knew what she was about, but I didn't. And that surprised me, because even then I considered myself good at being able to read someone's motives. It was a skill I had to learn to survive."

"What do you mean?"

"When I was a teenager, I trusted the wrong person, and I learned a hard lesson. I tried not to make that mistake again, but with Valerie I did just that."

"Who was that first person who abused your trust?"

He didn't answer right away, and she could see conflict in his eyes. "It was one of my foster parents. She wasn't who I thought."

"What did she do?"

"It doesn't matter now."

She hated that he'd cut her off just when things were getting interesting. But with Alex she had the sense that she had to tread carefully or he'd shut down completely.

"What about you?" he asked. "Were you in love with Doug?"

"I thought I was at the time."

"Anyone before him get your heart pounding?"

"I had a high school boyfriend that I adored, but we broke up after graduation, and he moved back east to college. He married someone he met there and I think they already have two kids."

"Did he break your heart?"

"He did," she admitted. "When you're sixteen, a lot of things break your heart. But I try to remember the good times. He was the first person who made me feel happy. For those years after my dad died, I was a little lost, and Charlie made me laugh. He was a funny guy, and he helped me not take my life so seriously."

"It seems like you could still use someone like that in your life," Alex suggested. "You seem to have a one-track mind, and it's all business."

"Not always all business," she reminded him, then was instantly sorry she'd gone down that road when an interested gleam entered his eyes. She cleared her throat. "Let's go back to your past. Did you have anyone in your life after your parents died that lessened the grief?"

"No, I didn't, not for a long time. But I couldn't worry about finding someone to like me; I was more concerned with surviving."

"It was that bad?"

"Yeah, it was that bad," he said grimly.

"Can you give me any examples?"

"I could, but I won't."

"Why not? Why can't you talk to me, Alex?"

"I am talking to you—I've been talking to you. My story has already been told, Andrea, by lots of other reporters, but you don't want that story. You want another one, one that will sell more magazines, one that doesn't exist. Maybe you should just make something up."

"I don't do that, Alex. And I'm just trying to understand you."

"You couldn't begin to understand my life. How could you? You grew up in a fairytale with a father you worshipped and a mother who baked cookies for you when you came home from school and a sister to share your secrets with." He placed his hands on his hips in a belligerent manner, daring her to defy his image of her. "Your biggest problem was probably trying to get your mother to let you wear makeup to school."

Andrea immediately shook her head. "You're more wrong than right, Alex. First of all, my mother loved for me to wear makeup, but I never did, because I was a tomboy. I cut off all my hair when I was eleven because I hated to brush it. Yes, my mother did bake cookies when I came home from school, and, yes, they were amazing, but our relationship was fraught with problems. My mother was always trying to turn me into herself. And I did worship my dad, but he was never around. I admired him greatly. He influenced my life. But the truth is that I barely knew him, and he barely knew me. He was always on the road, always working." She paused for breath. "I know what it feels like to lose a parent, maybe not two, but at least one. So don't try to tell me that there's no way I can understand your life," she finished.

"Did you really cut off your hair?"

She stared at him in amazement. "That's all you took out of what I just said?"

He shrugged. "I got stuck there."

"Yes, I cut it off with garden shears. My mother was so embarrassed she wouldn't go to the PTA meetings for a month. Even Laurel tried to disown me. She locked me in my room when she had a friend come over so I wouldn't be seen." She paused at his sudden smile. "It's not funny."

"Yes, it is. I didn't realize you were that impulsive."

"More like impatient. I used to swim, and when I got out of the pool, it took me an hour to get the tangles out of my long hair. It was painful, too. But I have to admit I looked pretty hideous after I cut it all off. My mother made me go to her hair stylist, who tried to make it look better, but we all just had to live with it for a few weeks." She took a breath. "I remember my mom on the phone with my dad, just ranting about how difficult I was, and how he should come home and help her raise me."

"Maybe that's really why you cut off your hair," Alex suggested.

"No." She wrinkled her brows as she thought about that. "I don't think I did it for that reason. No, it was just the tangles."

"If you say so," he said lightly.

"Now you tell me an embarrassing story," she ordered.

"Me? I don't have any of those. I was perfect."

"Think harder."

"Well, let's see. I was at a party in high school. One of those crazy big bashes where the parents aren't home and everyone is doing a lot of bad stuff."

"Go on."

"I had my eye on this girl. Her name was Shari. She was a cheerleader and a trust fund baby, definitely not someone who was going to look back at me, but I had a thing for her."

"What happened?"

"I drank a lot that night."

"Nothing good usually starts with that statement."

"So true. Shari told me she wanted to go skinny dipping in the pool, shock everyone, but she didn't want to do it by herself."

She groaned. "I think I know where this is going."

"Then you're smarter than me, because I had no clue. All I could think about was seeing her breasts, so I said, let's do it. I stripped down right there on the edge of the pool thinking she was right behind me. After I jumped into the pool, I came back up to see her fully dressed and laughing hysterically with a crowd of her friends."

She felt a wave of sympathy. "That's mean."

"What was even worse was that there was no way I could get out of the pool without showing everything off. I stayed in the water for an hour and a half. Which made things worse, because when I got out of the water…"

Laughing, she put her hand to her mouth as she shook her head. "That is really embarrassing."

"Yeah, you think? I was really happy when I had to change schools three months later. It was the one time I didn't mind being a new face in the classroom."

"Shari is kicking herself right now. She could have had a billionaire boyfriend. And she's probably fat, too."

"I have no idea where she is or what she looks like."

"We could find her on social media."

"I don't want to find her. I don't need to ever see her again."

"If it makes you feel any better, she might have seen that tabloid story about how well-endowed you are." She grinned as his eyebrows arched in surprise. "You didn't see that one? Apparently, some model you hooked up with in Paris told a reporter there that she'd never seen such an incredible—package."

He groaned. "No way. You're making that up. I have a PR department that follows my press around the world and I was never shown that article."

"Maybe they didn't want to embarrass you."

"Well, as you can see, I have nothing left to be embarrassed about."

"Actually, I haven't *seen* anything," she said, feeling a little reckless and wild.

A new gleam filled his eyes. "We can take care of that anytime." He grabbed her hands and pulled her up against his body. "But I need a little-warm up first."

As he kissed her, Andrea moved closer, sliding her hands under his t-shirt. She caressed the strong planes of his stomach, feeling the muscles clench under her fingers. He smelled like sweat and soap and everything masculine, and the growing hardness at her groin sent a ripping wave of desire through her.

She had never felt such a need for a man, a deep intense longing to be a part of someone. It felt raw and primitive, and she wanted to give in to the moment, to forget about everything but this man—his lips, his hands, his body on hers. She didn't want to just see him, she wanted to touch him, taste him, be with him in every possible way.

Alex's mouth left hers so suddenly she felt a rush of cold,

but then his lips trailed a hot path down her face to the curve of her neck, promising more, much more.

"How do you feel about dirt?" he asked in a rough, tender voice. "Because in another minute you're going to be flat on your back."

"Or maybe you will," she replied, meeting his gaze as he lifted his head. "I like to be on top."

He smiled down at her. "Of course you do."

"Do you have a problem with that?"

"You on top of me?" He shook his head. "Sounds like heaven. Tell me when and where."

His words reminded her that this sexy game was quickly getting out of hand. She licked her lips, as his gaze dared her to name a place, a moment. But how could she do that?

She let out a sigh and took a step back.

Disappointment flooded his gaze. She had a feeling the same emotion was showing in her eyes. She'd never been put in this position before. She'd never had to choose between doing her job and seeing someone. But it wasn't just the professional conflict. Deep down, she knew she couldn't take him up on his offer, because she was scared, because he made her dizzy and nervous and needy, and she didn't want to end up giving him everything and getting nothing in return.

"Andrea?" he questioned. "What are you thinking?"

"That we need to stop this."

"Enjoying each other?"

"Yes."

"I thought we were having fun."

"We were, but fun time is over."

"Because…"

"Because I can't have sex with you and write about you at the same time."

He nodded. "And…"

She frowned. "There doesn't have to be more. That's

enough."

"There is more," he said with a certainty she couldn't deny.

"Fine. You want me to say it—I'll say it. I don't want to get involved with you, because I don't want you to hurt me. You're way out of my league, like you and Shari. And I don't want to end up naked in the pool."

"I would never do that to you, Andrea. Never."

"Maybe not intentionally, not in a mean way, but I think you could hurt me, and I don't want to take that risk."

He gave her a long look, his eyes filled with emotions she couldn't decipher. "Fair enough. I wouldn't want to hurt you."

She blew out a breath at his response, not quite sure now how she felt about his acquiescence. She'd wanted him to say that he liked her, too, that he saw something in the future, long after the article was done. But he didn't say any of that. Why would he? They'd known each other for a couple of days, and he'd just been having fun with her.

She certainly seemed to be good at putting an end to fun, she thought, feeling a little annoyed with herself. Had she really needed to make such a big statement?

Too impulsive, once again.

Alex glanced down at his watch. "We both need to get to work."

"You go ahead. I'm going to take the way back a little slower."

"Are you sure?"

"Yeah. I'll be fine. I can go at my own pace and not hold you back."

Her words brought a frown to his mouth. She wanted to ask him what he was thinking now, but he took a quick turn and ran down the path.

As he disappeared around the next curve, she felt a sense of loss. Had she been wrong to push him away so quickly?

Would a casual relationship have been better than nothing?

She knew the answer to that—no.

She couldn't do casual with Alex, because she already liked him too much. She just wished he felt the same way, but it was clear now that he didn't. At least he hadn't lied to her. She supposed she should be grateful for that.

Chapter Ten

That afternoon Andrea realized that Alex had lied to her, maybe not about his feelings but about everything else. The information she'd just heard from her private investigator rang through her head like a clanging church bell at high noon.

"Hang on, Joe," she said, holding the phone away from her ear as she took a much-needed breath.

She stared bleakly out the window of the newsroom. The skyline of San Francisco met her gaze, the tall buildings standing out against a clear blue sky. At the edge of the city a blanket of fog was creeping in, ready to cover the city as day turned into night.

"Andrea, are you there?" Joe demanded. "Andrea?"

She put the phone back to her ear. "Sorry. Tell me again what you just said."

"There are no death records for Rose and Harold Donovan," he repeated. "The last address I have for Rose Donovan was in Los Angeles, California. At that time, Alex was nine years old and enrolled in the fourth grade at Carver Elementary School. The next time Alex appeared in my search was when he was ten years old and a ward of the state."

"He said he was twelve when his parents were killed in a crash."

"There's no record of a fatal car accident in Southern

California involving two people with the last name Donovan in the year in which Alex reported his parents' death," Joe reiterated.

"Maybe it didn't happen in California."

"He stated that that's where they were living when his parents died."

"If that's true, why didn't anyone else discover that Alex lied about his parents' death?"

"They must not have looked too hard," Joe said.

"What about Alex's aunt?"

"Alex went to live with a woman named Suzanne Banks while he was attending Kentmoor High School in Los Angeles. She was listed as his guardian on his high school records, but she was not a blood relation. Rose Donovan did not have a sister. She was an only child."

"Grandparents?"

"The grandparents on Alex's mother's side lived in Nebraska. The grandfather died when Alex was sixteen. The grandmother passed away when Alex was nineteen. But I couldn't find any contact between Alex and his grandparents."

"I wonder why they didn't come and get him when he ended up in foster care."

"A question probably only Alex can answer."

"What about his grandparents on his father's side?"

"Harold Donovan's parents were deceased when he was a child. Harold was a practicing dentist in Los Angeles until Alex was two years old. Then I lost complete track of him. There's no divorce record, no death certification, nothing."

"I don't understand, Joe. How do people just disappear? I thought everyone could be tracked through the Internet. The man lived somewhere at some point."

"I'm sure he did, but I haven't yet figured out where."

She was beginning to wonder just good of an investigator Joe was. He hadn't been able to track down her source on the car seat story, either. "So what's the next step?"

"I'll keep digging if you want."

"I do."

"Then I'll be in touch."

"Thanks." She set down the phone, thinking about what she'd learned. Why hadn't any other reporters found the holes in Alex's story? That was an easy answer—the only articles he had done were celebrity interviews, and they'd been more interested in who he'd slept with than anything else. Was this why he'd been so reticent to talk about his parents? But what did he have to hide? Why make up a lie about a car accident?

Getting up from her chair, she paced restlessly around her small cubicle, a dozen questions running through her head. She tried to remember everything Alex had told her about his parents and realized it amounted to nothing. Now she had a better understanding of why. The less he said, the fewer lies he would have to tell.

Pausing by her desk, she flipped through the clippings she'd collected and skimmed for any mention of his parents. Her gaze caught on one of the quotes. "My father was a dentist," Alex said. "That's why I have such great teeth. He taught me to floss when I was two."

She sat down in her chair, remembering Alex's conversation with his assistant a few days earlier when he'd been reminded to go to the dentist. Ellen had said something about Alex always cancelling dental appointments and that he hated to go to the dentist. That didn't jive with his love of flossing or the fact that his father was a dentist, unless, the fact that his father was a dentist had left some painful memories.

Or was she reading something into a nothing comment?

She had to figure out what Alex was hiding. Part of her wanted to confront him, see what he said when she told him what she'd found out, but first she would talk to Mick. She'd already gotten Liz and Kate to agree to take the self-defense class with her. Maybe afterward, she'd be able to pry some information out of Alex's old friend. It was a long shot, but it was all she had.

* * *

Alex was standing by the window of Mick's office when a car pulled into the alley in front of the gym and three women got out. One of them was an attractive blonde with a beautiful and very familiar face. His stomach turned over. What was Andrea doing here?

He'd been trying not to think about her since their run, but that hadn't been working too well. Every time he closed his eyes, her image came into his head. Every time he licked his lips, he was reminded of their kiss.

He stepped away from the window as the door opened behind him. For a moment he thought it might be Andrea, but Mick walked in.

Mick raised one eyebrow at his presence, then dropped a pile of towels on the chair in front of his desk. "What's up? You look like you just got a call from the IRS."

"I thought you were Andrea. I saw her get out of a car a second ago with some other women. What are they doing here?"

Mick cleared his throat. "Oh, did I mention that I'm starting a woman's self-defense class tonight?"

"No, you didn't."

"Really? I thought I had."

"And you invited Andrea?"

Mick nodded. "When she came to see me the other day. I need the business."

"She wants to quiz you for more information on me."

"Sure," Mick said easily. "But this way I get something out of it, too." He paused as a knock came at the door. "That's probably her. Are you ready?"

He shrugged. He was never really ready to see Andrea.

"Come in," Mick called out.

Andrea walked in with a cheerful smile, her blond hair pulled back into a ponytail on top of her head. She was dressed in sweats and a t-shirt, certainly nothing provocative, but Alex still felt a jangle at the end of every nerve. Unwilling to admit that she was getting to him, he growled at her, "What are you doing here?"

Her smile disappeared. "I'm taking a self-defense class from Mick. Do you have a problem with that?"

"As a matter of fact I do."

"Well, it's not your business," she retorted.

"Hold on," Mick interrupted. "If you two want to go a couple of rounds, I'll get you both some gloves, and we'll do it in the ring, not my office."

"I'm sorry," Andrea muttered, sending Alex a dark look. "He started it."

"You started it when you walked in here," Alex returned.

Mick sighed. "Did you want something Andrea?"

"No. I'll talk to you after class—when you're alone."

"Great," Mick said. "I need to get everyone signed in. I'll see you out there."

As Mick left the office, Alex shifted his feet and fought the urge to grab Andrea and kiss her until he didn't feel restless or needy anymore, but neither of those feelings was going to go away with one kiss.

He shoved his hands into his pockets. "What are you really doing here, Andrea? And don't tell me it's about self-defense class."

"It's partly about that, but I also wanted to talk to Mick about you, get some insight into your past."

"You don't need a middleman for that."

"Yes, I do. You get close and then you back away, and

I'm getting tired of the dance."

She had a point. He had been playing a game of push-pull, and it wasn't working, because every time he walked away from her, he wanted to go back. He needed to get this story done so he wouldn't have any reason whatsoever to see her.

"What do you want to know now?" he asked. "I thought I answered a lot of your questions this morning."

"Well, I'd really like to know why you lied to me about your parents' car accident."

He sucked in a quick breath. He'd wondered if she'd figure that out. He'd hoped not, but obviously Andrea was not to be underestimated.

"Why do you think I lied?" he countered.

"Because there's no record of their death." She held his gaze for a long moment. "Nothing to say?"

"Actually, I have a lot to say, but not here and not now. You have a class to get to, don't you?"

She frowned. "Yes, I do, and since I persuaded two of my friends to come with me, I really need to do it with them. Can we talk later tonight?"

"After class. I'll wait for you."

"Okay," she said, surprise in her eyes. "You're going to hang around for an hour? You don't have anything better to do?"

"I have a million better things to do, but I'll wait because you're right, we need to talk. We need to wrap this story up."

"My thoughts exactly. I'm glad we're finally on the same page."

He opened the door for her, and she preceded him down the hall and into one of the studios where Mick and a young guy were getting ready to start the class.

Alex sat down on a bench against the wall as Andrea joined a beautiful brunette that she addressed as Kate and a pretty blonde she called Liz. They were all quite attractive, but as the class progressed, their personalities also became apparent.

Andrea was a scrappy spitfire, Liz seemed cool, controlled and quite capable of delivering a lethal blow to any assailant, and Kate was a smiling, laughing girl, who seemed quite squeamish about violence. But it was hard not to like Kate. She was enthusiastic, if not very effective. Hopefully, none of them would ever have to actually defend themselves.

Andrea looked over at him every now and then, and he could barely take his eyes off of her. He really didn't know what to do about her. How much should he tell her? And more importantly how much information could he trust her with? The answer was very little. She was a reporter. She had a job to do. She wasn't going to leave something important out of her interview piece just because he asked nicely.

But even aside from the issue of the article, he didn't know what to do about her personally. She'd told him he could hurt her. He didn't want that to happen. He also didn't want her to hurt him. And that could happen, too. He hadn't let a woman get this close to him in a long time, especially a woman he hadn't slept with. But their emotional connection was as strong as the physical attraction, and in a few days she'd turned his life upside down. He couldn't imagine not seeing her again. On the other hand, where could any relationship with Andrea go?

No answer sprang to mind. He told himself to stop worrying about a relationship and focus on what he was going to tell her to hopefully derail her pursuit of his past. That was his most immediate problem.

He still hadn't figured that out when the class to an end.

He stood up as Andrea brought her friends over to meet him.

"Alex, these are two of my best friends, Kate Marlow and

Liz Palmer."

"Nice to meet you," Kate said, shaking his hand with a warm smile.

"Hello," Liz said, her smile more speculative than warm. "Andrea says she's writing a story about all your accomplishments."

"Yes, and I'm her least favorite assignment," he said lightly.

"I never said that," Andrea said quickly.

"Maybe not in so many words," he conceded. "But we both know you'd rather be interviewing a politician or a medical researcher or someone who's contributed greatly to the world."

"I don't know what you've done for the rest of the world," Kate interrupted. "But you've given me hours of escape and pleasure while playing your game SpookCraft. In fact, I don't think I could have gotten through calculus without it. I learned more about algebraic equations playing that game than I ever did in school."

He smiled. "Good to hear."

"What is SpookCraft?" Andrea asked.

"It's a spy game," Kate said, surprise in her voice. "Alex has sold millions of copies of it. It's been around for seven or eight years now. You didn't know that, Andrea?"

"There are so many games," Andrea said defensively.

"Well, you should know that one," Kate told her. "It's one of the top sellers. I used to try to get you to play it with me in college. Don't you remember?"

"Now that you mention it, I do remember. I just didn't know that was one of Alex's games."

"Almost every game we ever played was made by Alex's company," Liz said.

"I didn't realize," Andrea mumbled, looking a little embarrassed by the fact that her friends knew more about his games than she did. "We'll have to talk more about the games."

"We can do that now," he said.

"Yes," she agreed. Turning back to her friends, she said, "I'm going to catch a ride with Alex. I'll talk to you later."

As the women left, Alex said, "I like your friends."

"Because they play your games?"

"It's nice to know that I have a female audience."

"I suspect you always have a female audience, Alex," she said dryly. "But while I'll be happy to hear about your games, I want to talk about you tonight. Is that going to happen, or are you going to come up with another unexpected emergency?"

"I waited for you, didn't I? Let's go."

"All right."

They walked out to his car without further discussion. As Alex got behind the wheel, his phone rang. Tyler's number flashed across the screen. It was extremely unusual for Tyler to call instead of text. "I'm sorry, I have to get this." He answered his phone. "Hello, Tyler?"

"I need help."

"What's wrong?"

"I wrecked the Monroe's car. They were going to kick me out anyway, but now I'm done."

His stomach tightened. "Where are you?"

"I'm at Homer and Third. I started running and I couldn't stop, but now I don't know where to go. You can't take me back there, Alex. I just need bus money. I'll go away. I'll get out of everyone's hair."

"Just stay put. I'll be there in ten minutes. I mean it, Tyler. Don't move." He set down his phone. "I need to pick someone up."

"Who's Tyler?"

"A fourteen-year-old kid who probably just ruined his life."

"And how is he your problem?"

"I'm his mentor, his Big Brother. I need to go get him. Do you want to catch a cab home? Mick will call you one."

"No, I'm coming with you."

He didn't want to take her along, but he also didn't have time to argue.

"Go, Alex," Andrea said.

"All right."

As he pulled out of the alley, she said, "Tell me about Tyler."

"He's a foster kid and a good kid, most of the time."

"What's happening now?"

"He said something about wrecking the family car. He's too young to drive, so I don't know what the hell is going on. He's in a pretty good situation. I hate to think he's wrecked that."

"Well, it sounds like he's not physically hurt, if that's any comfort," she said with a sympathetic smile.

"It is. Thanks. I thought you'd give me a hard time for another unexpected emergency."

"This one sounds legitimate. It's nice of you to be a Big Brother, considering how busy you are running your company."

"I can relate to Tyler. I want to stop him from making the mistakes I made."

"What kind of mistakes?"

"I got so used to being sent away that sometimes I'd force the issue just so I wouldn't have to wait for it to happen. Tyler does the same thing. He tests the Monroes, pushes them to see how much they'll take. But they're a good family, and he could do a lot worse."

"Did you stay with any good families?"

"One, but then the mom got sick and the dad couldn't handle taking care of the kids, so we were split up and sent back into the system. The others ranged from nothing much to very bad. I ran away a bunch of times."

"And then you met someone you liked, who was willing to take you in, but she wasn't your aunt, was she?"

He gave Andrea a quick glance. "You have been digging, haven't you?"

She didn't answer, just gave him an expectant look.

"She wasn't my aunt. She was someone who had a big heart and was willing to take in a kid that no one else wanted."

"Thanks for finally telling me something that's true. That's a start."

"And that's all we're going to do for now," he said, as he neared their destination. "Before we pick up, Tyler, we need to get something straight. You cannot write about him. His name—this event—cannot be in your story. You have to promise me that. If you can't, I'm going to drop you off and get you a cab home."

She stared back at him. "I will keep Tyler out of the article. That's a promise."

"Okay, good."

"But you and I still have a lot more to talk about."

Chapter Eleven

Andrea settled back in her seat as Alex drove slowly through another run-down neighborhood. A couple of homeless people were camped in a doorway, and the shops all had bars over the windows. It was eight o'clock at night and everything but a nearby liquor store was closed.

"There he is," Alex said, relief in his voice.

She saw a lone figure standing in the shadow of a building.

"Stay here, Andrea. And keep the doors locked."

"Okay." Andrea watched as Alex walked over to the boy. The kid was wearing a baseball cap, a T-shirt and jeans, and he had a backpack over his shoulders.

Alex put a hand on the boy's arm. Whatever he was saying was making Tyler very uncomfortable. He kept looking at the ground and shuffling his feet. Once in a while he tried to make his own argument, but whatever he was saying appeared to be quickly taken apart by Alex.

As her gaze moved down the street, she noticed two older boys walking toward Alex and Tyler. She tensed, suddenly seeing Alex in the glare of the streetlight as they did—a prime, juicy target. His car and his suit cried money, a beacon calling out to the youths. It didn't take long before they moved.

Andrea's only thought was to warn Alex. She forgot about

his admonition to stay in the car with the doors locked. She had never been a passive bystander, and she wouldn't be one now.

She jumped out of the car and yelled, "Alex."

Her voice brought everyone's attention to her.

Alex turned toward her, but he was further away than the two guys, one of whom grabbed her, wrapping his arm around her neck.

A surge of panic ran through her as she struggled in his hold.

"Stay back," the other guy warned Alex as he took a step forward.

"Tyler, get in the car," Alex said sharply.

Tyler took a wide berth around the group as he ran toward the car.

"Let go of her," Alex demanded.

"Give me your wallet," the other man said to Alex. "Toss it over here."

Alex hesitated and then took out his wallet and tossed it to the guy.

"Not bad," the kid said, whistling under his breath as he opened the billfold. "Jackpot." As he held up the wad of cash to show his friend, the grip on her neck loosened.

She knew she had one second to use it to her advantage. Remembering what Mick had just taught her, she kicked hard at the guy's shin and managed to throw him off balance. She gave him a shove backward, and he tumbled to the ground, hitting his head on the pavement and knocking himself out.

At her move, Alex had jumped the other guy, and they were now fighting. Alex dodged one punch, but the second one connected with face.

Alex threw a hard fist, and the kid staggered, but came back swinging. She looked around for some kind of weapon, some way to help. But there was nothing and no one in sight.

Finally, Alex shoved the kid against the wall as sirens lit up the air.

Within minutes, two police cars had pulled up, four officers jumping out to take charge of the situation. Alex released the kid and walked over to her.

He gave her a quick hug and a worried, searching look. "Are you okay?"

"I'm good," she said, her voice more shaky than she would have liked.

"You're more than good, you're amazing. You would have made Mick proud at that move you made."

"I guess I'm lucky I just came from class. It was fresh in my mind."

They broke apart as the police came to take their statements. An ambulance arrived to deliver one of the assailants to the hospital while the other one was handcuffed and put into the back of a police car. Then they were told they were free to leave.

"I'm sorry," Tyler said as they approached the car. He was standing by the door, a guilty look on his face. "This is my fault."

"Not at all," Alex said with a firm shake of his head. "We were just in the wrong place at the wrong time."

"Because I called you," Tyler said. "I mess everything up."

"This isn't on you. The rest of it—maybe—but not this. You take responsibility for what you do, not what others do. Now get in the car." As Alex reached for the door handle, he winced. He raised his left hand and gave it a bemused look. "Andrea, I think you're going to have to drive."

She stared at his swollen wrist in amazement. "Oh my God, Alex. It looks like your hand is broken. Why didn't you tell the police you needed medical help?"

"Because I don't need an ambulance. Maybe just a ride to

the E.R."

"You are definitely going to the hospital," she said taking the keys out of his good hand. "Let's go."

She slid behind the wheel as Alex got in the front seat and Tyler slid into the back. "I hope your hand isn't broken."

"If it is, it will heal," he said pragmatically.

"You beat the shit out of that guy," Tyler interjected, awe in his young voice. "I thought you were dead. That's why I called the cops."

"That was the smartest thing you've done today." Alex shifted in his seat, flinging Tyler another look. "Now tell me what happened at your house?"

Tyler hesitated. "I was sitting in the car waiting for Joan to come out. The keys were in the ignition, and I was just thinking it would be cool to be able to drive wherever I wanted to go. So I moved behind the wheel, and I started the car. I wasn't going to do anything or go anywhere. Then the stupid cat jumped on the hood and distracted me. I hit the gas, and I accidentally drove through the garage door."

"Was anyone hurt?"

"No, but Joan was pissed. She came running out of the house screaming at me. I got out of the car and I ran down the block, and I didn't stop."

"Tyler," Alex said with a sigh. "You can't run away. You have to make this right."

"It doesn't matter what I do. They're going to get rid of me anyway. They're having a baby. I heard them talking the other day. They're finally going to get their own kid. You know what that means."

"Not necessarily," Alex said slowly. "You need to talk to them, and so do I. They're probably worried sick about you."

As Alex shifted, trying to reach his phone, Andrea saw the pain in his eyes. "Alex, you can wait to call them until you get to the hospital. Try to keep your hand elevated."

"All right, but I am going to call them." He gave Tyler a hard look. "And you are done running, all right? Don't make me chase after you."

"I won't," Tyler promised. "Maybe you could let me live at your house."

"We'll talk options later," Alex said. "The Monroes are a good family."

"Yeah, but I'm not in their family. I'm not their blood, not like this new kid is going to be."

Tyler fell silent as they pulled into the hospital parking lot. Andrea stopped the car at the door. "You can get out here. I'll park, and then Tyler and I will come in."

Alex didn't look like he cared for that scenario, but she knew he didn't have much choice. He couldn't leave Tyler alone, and right now she was the only one available to look out for the kid.

"Thanks, sorry about this."

"It's not a problem."

As Alex entered the hospital, she drove into the lot and parked the car. "I'm Andrea by the way," she said as she and Tyler got out of the car.

By the time they arrived at the lobby, Alex was already in an examination room, leaving Andrea and Tyler in the waiting room. It was the perfect time for her to pump the kid for information. He knew Alex better than she did. But Tyler was obviously worried about Alex, and she couldn't bring herself to take advantage of his vulnerability. It sounded like he had a lot of his own problems to deal with.

"How about something to drink?" she asked him. "Maybe a snack? I think Alex will be awhile."

"I am kind of hungry," Tyler muttered.

"Then let's go down to the cafeteria."

"Are you Alex's girlfriend?"

"No. I'm just a friend." As she said the words, she realized she didn't want to be Alex's friend or the reporter writing a story about him. But she didn't know how to be anything else, and more importantly, she didn't know if Alex wanted her to be anything else.

Even if he did, how could she contemplate getting involved with someone who had lied to her and to everyone else? She couldn't end up with another Doug. She had to be smart.

But she also wanted to give Alex a chance to explain. Before they were done with each other, she was going to know every last one of his secrets.

* * *

Andrea was probably grilling Tyler for information, Alex thought as the nurse stuck a needle deep into his arm, blending an immediate shaft of pain with numbing relief. He tried to remember just what Tyler knew about his past, but his brain was spinning from the adrenaline rush, the pain, and now the drugs, and he couldn't think straight. Nor could he do anything about the situation. He was stuck here until his broken hand was put in a cast, which was going to take some time.

In between visits from the doctor and the nurse, he managed to call Tyler's foster parents and explain the situation. Joan Monroe, Tyler's foster mother, wasn't angry, just very worried. When Alex told her that Tyler was concerned about his place in the family with a new baby possibly on the way, Joan started to cry, saying she loved Tyler. She didn't want to lose him. She wanted to adopt him whether or not a baby came along as well.

Alex was very happy to hear her honest and emotional words. The Monroes would do right by Tyler. Tyler just had to give them a chance.

He told Joan that he'd keep Tyler at his house for the night just to give them all a little breathing room. Then he'd take him to school in the morning, and tomorrow afternoon they could all sit down together.

After ending that call, he settled back on the exam table and stared at the ceiling, his body still tense with all the emotions that had run through him the past hour. When he'd seen that man grab Andrea, he'd been filled with anger and also terrified that he wouldn't be able to protect her. But she'd defended herself. She was a smart, gutsy woman, who didn't back down from a fight. She'd jumped out of the car to warn him, no thought to her own safety.

She was one hell of a woman.

The kind of woman he could respect.

The kind of woman he could love.

He tensed at that thought.

He couldn't allow the word *love* into his vocabulary. It was the gateway to pain, and he'd had enough pain. A voice inside his head suggested that Andrea might be worth the risk. But he had other things to worry about besides love. He couldn't forget that Andrea had the potential to destroy more than a few people. She knew he'd lied about his parents dying in a car accident. He needed to stop her from finding out the rest.

* * *

By the time his wrist was set in a cast and he was released from the hospital, nearly two hours had passed. It was almost eleven when a nurse wheeled him into the waiting room. Andrea was reading something on her phone while Tyler was sprawled across two chairs and fast asleep.

Andrea immediately got to her feet when she saw him.

He tried not to look too closely at her, not wanting to let any of his hard-built resolutions of the past two hours get tarnished by a tender look. But when she touched the side of his face, tracing the bruise by his eye, his good hand went up to catch hers and he found himself letting her continue the gentle movement rather than pushing her away.

"Are you okay?" she asked.

"I'll live. I just have a new accessory," he said, holding up his cast.

"At least you have a good story to go with it. You were quite the hero tonight."

"I think that could be said about you."

She shook her head. "I should have called the cops instead of jumping out of the car. That would have been the smarter thing to do."

"But you saw trouble, and you had to help."

"It's a bad habit of mine to act first and think later," she said.

"Most people are content to let someone else help out, but not you. I like that about you."

"Well, thanks. Does your hand hurt?"

"Right now I feel damn good," he said, his words slurring together.

She smiled. "Let's get you home."

"Good idea. By the way, I called Tyler's foster parents and told them he'd stay with me tonight."

"He'll be happy about that. He's worried about whatever punishment is coming his way."

"That's good. I want him to worry. Hopefully, he won't do anything so stupid again." Alex got up from the wheelchair and walked over to Tyler. Tapping him on the shoulder, he said, "Hey, kid. Time to go home."

Tyler blinked his eyes and gave him a sleepy look. "Are you finally done?"

"Yeah, and I talked to the Monroes. You can stay with me tonight."

Relief flashed in Tyler's eyes as he got to his feet. "Thanks. What about what I did to the garage?"

"We'll talk about that tomorrow."

"Okay."

They walked out to the car, and Andrea once again slid behind the wheel.

Alex yawned as he buckled his seat belt. He had a feeling he would be asleep before they were out of the parking lot.

"Do you remember how to get to my house?" he asked, his eyes very heavy.

"Yes. Just rest. Let me take care of you tonight."

"That sounds nice. I can't remember when I last let that happen."

* * *

During the quiet drive home, Andrea was filled with mixed emotions. The evening had certainly not turned out as she had planned. She still had questions to ask Alex. She needed to know why he'd lied to her and to the rest of the world. But at the moment she just wanted to take care of him, which was an unexpected feeling. She'd never really thought of herself as a nurturer. That was a title better suited to her sister or her mom. But with Alex, she felt so many things. He could make her hot, make her crazy, and make her feel incredibly emotional and protective.

She had the scary thought that maybe this was what love felt like.

Glancing over at him, her heart twisted once again. At the moment, he was not rich, powerful and in charge. Instead, he was vulnerable. His shirt was splattered with dirt and blood. The bruise around his eye was puffy and turning a dark purple, and his hand looked as fat as a watermelon in a white cast. He was definitely off his game. The guard walls were down. He might be a sexy playboy millionaire most days, but tonight he was just a man in pain, and she was going to take care of him.

When they arrived at Alex's home, she and Tyler helped a very sleepy and dazed Alex into the house. Fortunately, Tyler seemed to know where Alex's bedroom was, so she didn't have to waste time figuring out which of the six bedrooms belonged to him.

After they got Alex onto his bed, Tyler said he was going to sleep in the room he usually used.

She followed Tyler down the hall, pausing at the door of his bedroom. She couldn't help noting that the furnishings were very teenage male: a queen-sized bed with a dark blue comforter, a TV on one wall as well as a video game box on a nearby table. A desk with a computer was by the window, and there were posters from Alex's games on the walls.

"Do you stay here a lot?" she asked curiously.

"Once a month," Tyler replied. "I wish I could live here all the time. And not just because Alex gives me stuff. He's just really cool. And he gets me."

She nodded. "I know he cares a lot about you, Tyler."

"He's still going to send me back to the Monroes."

"Well, you can talk to him about that tomorrow. I know that Alex wants to do right by you, and I think you have to trust him to know what that is."

"Yeah, okay. Thanks for buying me dinner, Andrea."

"Any time."

"Are you going to be here in the morning?"

She hesitated. "I'm not sure yet. Maybe."

He nodded. "You should stay. Alex likes you."

Her heart turned over at the simple words. "I like him, too."

"Are you sure you're not his girlfriend?"

"Our relationship is complicated."

"If you both like each other, what's the problem?"

She couldn't begin to answer that question. "Goodnight, Tyler."

After shutting his bedroom door, she wandered down the hall, curious about the other bedrooms. Alex had obviously had Tyler's room decorated with a teenage boy in mind. Did any other strays occasionally spend the night in his house?

She found her answer in the next room. There were twin beds with pink and white comforters, white bookshelves and desks, and floral curtains on the windows. It was a dream room for a girl or two girls, and she couldn't help wondering who had occupied this room.

Closing the door, she checked the rest of the rooms, finding nothing but ordinary guestrooms.

She returned to the master bedroom and saw Alex sprawled out on the bed. He didn't look very comfortable in his clothes, but there was no way she was going to attempt to undress him. She could at least take off his shoes and maybe his tie so he didn't strangle himself.

The shoes came off easily. The tie slipped off his neck, and she managed to undo the buttons of his shirt without any problem. When she got to his waist, she pulled the ends of his shirt out of his pants. The belt was a bit more of a challenge. She released the buckle and started to pull it through the loops, but Alex moved, his shirt coming completely open, and she was now staring at his solid, tanned chest. There was a smattering of dark hair covering the well-defined muscles of his chest and stomach, disappearing in a line below his waistband.

She flushed as her imagination completed the picture. What on earth was wrong with her? She had seen naked men before. But this half-dressed unconscious man sent her pulses racing.

Her fingers lingered on his belt buckle as her eyes traveled up his chest, to the strong jaw, the generous curve of his mouth, the amused grin in his eyes, the spark of desire.

Oh, Lord, he was awake.

"Are you taking off my pants?" His voice was a bit dazed, and Andrea suddenly realized that her fingers were playing with the snap on his waistband.

"I was just getting your belt off to make you more comfortable, so you could sleep."

Alex suddenly shifted, and his good hand came around her back, pulling her down on top of him. The amusement in his eyes faded into something darker and more dangerous.

"Andrea," he murmured, his husky voice turning her name into an intimate caress. "I've dreamed of having you here in my bed."

She stared at him, mesmerized by his tone, the hungry look in his eyes, the pulse working a rapid beat in his neck. She didn't resist when he pulled her face down to his. She was helpless, a victim of her own desire. He kissed her deeply, passionately, sliding his tongue into her mouth, demanding a response as his hand ran down the length of her spine, making her arch like a cat.

He wasn't holding her anymore, but she couldn't move away. Just one more kiss, one more moment, maybe two, and then she would stop.

His mouth worked its magic, his body stiffening against hers, making her aware of their intimate position. She braced herself on her hands and slowly pulled away, her breath coming in ragged gasps.

Alex stared at her. "Don't go, Andrea. Stay with me."

It was really tempting, but while Alex was in a daze, she knew exactly what was going on. She also knew that sleeping with Alex with so much unresolved between them was not the right thing to do, no matter how much she wanted it.

"I can't," she whispered.

There was a light in his eyes, almost a fever. It burned

right through her, tempting her again, making her want to forget everything but the desire that was pulling them together.

"I need you," he murmured.

"You don't know what you're saying." She sat back on her knees, looking down at him. He dropped his hand from her hair to his side, a look of pain turning his light green eyes to jade.

"Don't leave me. I can't take it. I just can't." His eyes drifted closed, and his breathing changed to one of slumber.

Andrea stared at him, touched by the depth of pain in his voice. This man had been hurt badly in his life. She only knew bits and pieces of his story, but that was one inescapable truth.

She'd been worried about him hurting her, but she could hurt him, too, she realized. She rolled over onto her side, propping her head on her elbow as she stared at his strong, handsome face. She didn't want to think about the article right now or all the lies between them. She just wanted to be with him.

Kicking off her shoes, she pulled up a quilt from the bottom of the bed and covered them both. She would just stay with him for a little while. In case his hand hurt. In case he needed her. Just a few minutes...

Chapter Twelve

The sunlight streaming through the window drew Alex out of a deep sleep. When he tried to move, his body felt bruised and heavy, as if there was a large weight on his chest. He blinked one eye open, then the other. Then he blinked again, unable to believe what he was seeing.

His other senses immediately clicked in. Blond hair tickled the bare skin on his chest. A slender leg intertwined with his, causing an immediate reaction in another part of his body.

Andrea was in bed with him!

It didn't seem possible. It had to be a dream—a bright, vivid dream. But he could smell the scent of her shampoo, see the dark lashes curving down against her cheek, and her expression was that of a sweet, sexy angel.

He shook his head and closed his eyes again, but when he took another look she was still there. A heavy fog filled his mind as he tried to make sense of the obvious. They had gone to bed together, and he didn't remember a damn thing. Why?

He groaned as he moved his arm, and the memories of the past evening came flooding back. He remembered getting into the car after leaving the hospital and that was it.

Somehow Andrea and Tyler must have gotten him into the house and up the stairs. But that didn't explain why Andrea had climbed into bed with him, why she had slept with him instead of going home or just using one of the guest rooms.

He shifted slightly, hoping she wouldn't wake up. Now that he was alert, he wanted to take a better look.

Asleep, Andrea looked a lot softer, less energized, ambitious and determined. She was such a fighter when she was awake, but now she appeared relaxed, content. Her skin was clear and smooth with just a few laugh lines around the corners of her eyes. He smiled, thinking of her open, charming grin, the laughter that would reach her eyes, even when she tried to be serious.

She would hate the fact that he was watching her, seeing her off guard without all her defenses in place. He smiled to himself, enjoying the way her arm curved around his waist. It felt good, too damn good. He didn't want her to wake up. He wanted her to hold him forever. But even as the thought came to mind, she gently began to stir, waking up in slow, uneasy stages that brought indistinguishable murmurs to her lips.

He liked the way she fought off the morning. It was in keeping with the way she resisted him, an inevitable, futile struggle against what was meant to be, although, what was meant to be probably shouldn't be. Andrea had already discovered some of his lies. She wouldn't stop until she'd stripped him bare.

He wanted her to strip him bare, just not that way.

Finally, Andrea's eyes opened, and she stared at him, at first blankly, and then with a dawning sense of awareness and embarrassment. She raised her head and then pushed herself into a sitting position, her hair falling out of her ponytail in wild abandon.

He pushed a strand back behind one ear. "I'm glad you finally decided to sleep with me."

"We didn't sleep together. Well, we did sleep, but nothing else," she muttered. "So, you're awake."

He grinned. "And so are you."

"You're probably wondering what I'm doing in bed with you."

He propped himself up on the pillows. "Actually, I'm just hoping you'll stay."

"I was worried about you. I didn't think you should be left alone. I was just going to rest for a minute, but I fell asleep."

"I'm not angry, Andrea."

"Well, I don't want you to read anything into this."

"Into the fact that we're in bed together? That you were wrapped up around me while you slept? Why would I read into that?"

Her cheeks flushed a pretty pink. "I'm always a little restless when I sleep."

"I'll keep that in mind the next time."

"There's not going to be a next time, Alex." She blew out a breath. "How's your hand?"

"It hurts," he said, admitting the truth.

"You probably need another painkiller."

"Maybe a kiss would do the trick."

She frowned. "You never quit flirting, do you?"

Her question drove the smile off of his face. "That's not what I'm doing."

"It's not?"

He stared back at her, wanting to say so many things, but in the end he said nothing.

"I should get up," she said finally.

"Where's Tyler?"

"Probably asleep."

He glanced at the clock by the bed. It was seven. He had promised Tyler's foster parents that he would get him to school. "We have to get up. I have to drive him to school."

"I don't think you're going to be driving anywhere today."

"I can manage with one hand," he muttered.

A door slammed down the hall, and she jumped off the bed. "Tyler is awake."

"Don't worry. He won't come in here without knocking."

"I can't imagine what he would think if he saw me in here. Actually, I can imagine. He already asked me if I was your girlfriend."

"What did you tell him?"

"No, of course."

"Did he believe you?"

She made a face. "Not really."

He smiled. "Smart kid. He knows there's something going on between us—so do you."

"I can't have this conversation before coffee," she said with a shake of her head.

"Why don't you make us both some?" he suggested as she headed toward the door.

"All right. Do you need anything else?"

He sat up and swung his legs off the side of the bed, unable to repress a murmur of pain as he did so.

She immediately came back to him. "Are you okay?"

"I'll be fine. Just make some coffee and see if Tyler needs anything."

"All right. I'd tell you to call out if you need my help, but I doubt you would, so I'll save myself the trouble. You're stubbornly independent, Alex."

"I have a feeling people say that about you."

"Well, we're not talking about me." She paused. "I don't think you can take a shower with that cast."

"I've got a big tub."

"Well, try not to fall in the bath. I really don't want to spend another day in the Emergency Room."

"You could join me, make sure that doesn't happen," he teased.

She made a face at him. "I'll see you downstairs."

* * *

Andrea took the stairs two at a time, jogging down to the first floor so she wouldn't do something stupid like get into that bath with Alex. He had a way of bringing out her wild side and to hell with her conscience.

When she entered the kitchen, she found Tyler eating a bowl of cereal at the kitchen counter and watching some cop show re-run on the flat screen TV hanging on the wall.

She smiled. "Morning. I see you got something to eat."

"Alex always says to help myself."

"Then I guess it's a good thing that you did." She walked around the island in the kitchen and stared at the clean, granite-topped counters. Somewhere in the mass of cabinets was a coffeemaker and probably some food, but where?

Tyler pointed to a cupboard by the refrigerator. "Cereal is in there if you want some."

"Thanks, but I was looking for a coffeemaker."

"Over there." Tyler motioned to the other side of the room, and Andrea followed his instructions to find the most complicated-looking coffeemaker she had ever seen in her life.

"It figures," she mumbled to herself, eyeing the thing with a grouchy frown. Alex Donovan would have to have the most deluxe equipment possible. She plugged it in and read the directions. Then she ground the beans, poured in water, punched a few buttons and hoped for the best. The opening drops looked promising, a dark, rich brown in color. As the pot began to fill, a pleasant aroma filled the room.

With a triumphant smile, she walked over to the refrigerator and examined the contents. Eggs, milk, butter. She could definitely handle scrambled eggs, maybe some toast. And there was always cereal.

By the time Alex came down the stairs, she had breakfast

almost ready and was pleasantly awaiting his surprised expression. Not that she was trying to impress him. She had never bought into her mother's theory that any man worth having was worth cooking for. Still, it would be nice to know she could do it if she wanted to. And for some reason she did want to. Which made her a little worried that she was losing her focus. Her career had always meant everything to her. Now she was starting to want more.

"Smells good," Alex commented, sniffing the air.

She poured him a cup of coffee. "Cream? Sugar? Sweetener?"

"Black is fine."

She handed Alex his coffee. He took a sip and then walked over to the sink and spit it out.

She stared at him in astonishment. "Is it that bad?"

"Did you try it?"

"No, but it smells right."

He handed her the cup. Go ahead, take a sip."

After seeing Alex's display, she allowed only a small portion into her mouth, immediately gagging at the thick, chunky quality of the liquid. He was right. It was ghastly. She followed his lead and spit it out into the sink, then turned on the faucet and dumped out the rest of the cup. "Sorry. These million-dollar gadgets are a little beyond my experience."

"Andrea, the eggs..." Tyler's voice sent her attention to the stove cut where her scrambled eggs were now burning.

She quickly moved the pan and turned off the flame, but it was too late. "Sorry, I'm a lousy cook," she said with a sigh.

"Well, I'm not," Alex replied. "I'm pretty good. Let me show you."

"You're going to cook for me with one hand in a cast?" she asked doubtfully.

"Why don't we do it together?" he suggested.

"Okay, what do you want me to do?"

Making breakfast with Alex was more fun than she'd expected. She did most of the work while he gave instructions, but in the end they had beautiful golden pancakes, freshly squeezed orange juice and delicious chunks of cut-up fruit. The conversation over breakfast was light and easy, all of them choosing to stay away from uncomfortable topics.

"There are more pancakes in the oven," Alex reminded her, as she finished her last bite.

"Are you telling me that as a warning not to try to get anything off your plate?" she teased.

"Just pointing out that we have more food," he said evenly.

"Alex hates to share," Tyler interjected. "He won't even give me any of his popcorn when we go to the movies. He always makes me get my own."

"So you get enough," Alex replied, his lips turning down into a frown. "I don't think my eating habits need to be discussed."

Andrea rested her elbows on the table. "What's the big deal about guarding your food, Alex? Is that some primitive territorial urge? Or does it date back to your past, when maybe you didn't have enough to eat?"

"There was a time when I didn't know where my next meal was coming from," he admitted.

"And that feeling has never gone away?"

"I haven't really thought about it." Alex turned to Tyler. "I told the Monroes I'd take you to school. Do you need to stop by your house first to get anything?"

Tyler shook his head. "I have what I need."

"Then we should leave soon. Why don't you run a comb through your hair, maybe brush your teeth."

Tyler groaned but got up from the table, put his cereal bowl in the sink and then headed upstairs.

"You'd make a good parent, Alex," she commented.

"It's not hard to parent for a few minutes a day. But I'm not Tyler's father, just his friend."

"You're more than his friend. He adores you. He looks up to you, and he wants to be just like you."

"I hope I provide a good example."

"Of course you do." She drew in a breath, knowing it was time to cut to the chase. "Alex, we have to talk."

"I have to take Tyler to school in a few minutes."

"You can't keep putting me off."

"I'm just stating a fact."

"Well, we have a few minutes," she said with determination. "Why did you lie to me about your parents dying in a car accident?"

He let out a heavy sigh. "I first gave that answer about eight years ago. Someone threw the question out at me, and that seemed the simplest explanation. Once it was in print, I let it go."

"How did they die?"

"I don't want to talk about it."

She stared at him in frustration. "You told me you would answer my questions."

"Why does it matter?" he countered. "My parents are not responsible for the man I am today. They were gone a long time ago. I am a self-made man, and that's the story I want you to write, because that's the truth. I built my business from nothing. I achieved my goals, and I give back wherever I can. Why isn't that enough for you?"

She ignored his question. "Who sleeps in the pink and white bedroom upstairs that looks like a little girl's dream room?"

The color drained from his face. "You snooped around my house when I was asleep?"

"Yes," she admitted. "And once again you haven't answered my question."

"It was furnished for some girls I thought might be coming to visit, but they didn't. End of story."

She didn't think they were anywhere close to the end of his story. In fact, they were finally beginning. "What girls? Are they relatives? Are they like Tyler—kids who need a parental role model?" She paused. "Are they your daughters?"

"No!" he said vehemently. "Why would you ask me that?"

"It's not an illogical question."

"I don't have any children, Andrea. Are we done?"

"You know we're not."

He looked back at her, all warmth gone from his eyes. "Well, we're finished for now. I'm going to drive Tyler to school. I'll call you a cab."

"We could talk after you drop him off."

"No, we can't," he said firmly. "I have meetings at the office."

She had no idea if that was true or just another stall, but Alex was up and out of the room before she could say another word.

She cleared the table, rinsing the dishes and putting them in the dishwasher. She was just wiping down the counter when Alex's phone began to buzz. She glanced over at it, seeing a text message that made her heart skip a beat.

I'll be at Pier 39 at four o'clock in front of the carousel. Please come. Mom.

Mom?

She was stunned at the three-letter word.

Alex's mother was dead. Wasn't she?

She jumped as the kitchen door opened, but it wasn't Alex, it was Tyler.

"Alex wanted me to grab his phone and tell you that a car service will meet you out front in five minutes. He said just to shut the door behind you. It automatically locks."

"Okay," she mumbled as Tyler picked up Alex's phone

and left the kitchen.

She wondered what Alex would do when he saw the message. Although, he obviously knew his mother was alive, and they had some contact with each other, if she had his cell phone number. So what was going on?

She'd given Alex every opportunity to tell her the truth. Maybe it was time to find out for herself.

Chapter Thirteen

It felt wrong, Andrea thought several hours later as she walked toward Pier 39 just before four o'clock. But she couldn't stop herself from moving forward. The carousel beckoned. The chance to meet Alex's mother or at least see her was impossible to resist. But she still had no idea what she would do when she got there. If Alex saw her, he'd be furious. He'd know she'd read his private message. But it wasn't like she'd gone through his phone. The text had flashed right in front of her. How could she not have read it?

Well, maybe she could have, but what was done was done. And she was too good of a reporter not to follow a lead. Unfortunately, Alex was more than a story. He was a friend. He was someone she cared about.

This was exactly why she shouldn't have gotten personally involved with him. Her feelings were clouding her professional judgment. She'd always known exactly what to do—until now.

She walked down the pier toward the carousel, still debating her options.

An older woman with dark hair stood in front of the carousel, her gaze darting every which way as if she were looking for someone. Tall and slender, she was the feminine version of Alex. She appeared to be in her early fifties and was obviously well-off, judging by the large diamond ring on her third finger, the one she was tapping nervously against her designer bag.

The details didn't make sense. Alex had supposedly grown up in foster care. If his mother wasn't dead, where had she been? And if she had money, why would Alex have ended up in the system?

The questions continued to race through her mind with every step. Finally, Andrea took a deep breath and walked over to the woman. "Mrs. Donovan?"

The woman flinched. "I haven't been Mrs. Donovan in a long time. Who are you?"

"Andrea Blain. I saw your text to Alex this morning, and I wanted to meet you."

"Why? Are you his girlfriend?"

"No. I'm just a friend."

"Is he coming to meet me? Or did he send you in his place?"

"I'm not sure if he's coming," she said evasively. It was quite possible Alex could show up at any moment.

Disappointment and pain filled her eyes. "He probably won't come. He never has before. Why should this time be different?"

"You've asked him to meet you before?"

"Dozens of times. I keep hoping one day he'll show up." Alex's mother paused. "Why are you here?"

She decided to tell the truth. "I'm a reporter. I'm doing an article on Alex, and when I saw your text, I knew I had to talk to you, because Alex told me you were dead. Obviously, you're not."

The woman's expression turned wary. "You're a reporter?"

"Yes for *World News Today*. We're doing an in-depth story on Alex. He's our *Man of the Year*."

"Well, imagine that—*Man of the Year*." The woman sighed. "I always knew he was going to be somebody. He had that drive even when he was a little kid." She paused, cocking her head to the right. "Alex is still telling everyone I'm dead? I thought he would have dropped the story by now. But to Alex, I probably am dead."

"Why?" As soon as the word came out of her mouth, Andrea knew she couldn't do it. "Wait, don't answer that."

"Why not?" the woman asked in surprise.

"I can't let you tell me. Alex has to be the one. This doesn't feel right. I'm sorry. I shouldn't have come here. I hope Alex meets you, but I have to go."

"Wait. Will you give him this?" Alex's mother opened her bag and pulled out an envelope. "I wrote it just in case he wouldn't stay long enough to listen to what I had to say."

She hesitated. If she took the envelope, she'd have to tell Alex she'd met his mother, and he would be furious. On the other hand, she probably couldn't and shouldn't keep this visit a secret.

"Please?" his mother begged. "It's so hard for me to get him to listen. Maybe he'll read this and he'll be able to understand."

She wondered exactly what Alex had to understand. "All right," she agreed. "I'll make sure he gets your letter."

"Thank you. It probably won't make a difference, but at least I will have tried."

* * *

Alex got home a little after four, having spent a couple of pointless hours at his office before picking up Tyler and meeting with the Monroes. That situation now seemed to be settled, at least for the moment. He tossed his keys onto the side table and walked into his den. He grabbed a beer from behind the bar and sat down on the couch, propping his feet up on the coffee table. His entire body ached from yesterday's fine, and his hand had been throbbing for the last hour. But the physical pains weren't the reason for his frustration and restlessness—that was all Andrea.

It was only a matter of time before she'd be back with more questions. He'd hoped he could persuade her that his past had nothing to do with his present. But since she'd caught him in a lie, her curiosity was even more engaged. She really was a bulldog.

The doorbell rang, as if on cue, and he got up to answer it, knowing that there could be no more stalling. The moment of truth had arrived.

He opened the door. "Andrea."

She gave him a tentative smile. "Hi."

He wished his heart didn't jump every time he laid eyes on her. It would be easier for him if he could see her like an enemy and not like a woman he wanted to sleep with. She'd changed her clothes since he'd last seen her, now wearing skinny jeans and a button-down sweater over a silky top. Her hair flowed around her shoulders and her eyes were bright. He didn't know if it was worry or anger that put the light in her eyes. She was definitely feeling conflicted about something.

"Can I come in?" she asked.

He stepped back. "Of course. I'm glad you came back." Despite the fact that she was here to rip his life apart, he was still inexplicably happy to see her, which told him just how far gone he was.

Andrea seemed to find his statement difficult to believe. "You're happy I'm here? You couldn't get rid of me fast enough this morning."

He tipped his head. "I've had time to think since then." And what he'd realized was that he was going to have to tell her something—enough to satisfy her curiosity so she would stop looking for more lies. He didn't care about most of his past, but there was one part he still needed to protect.

He led her down the hall to his den. It was where he spent most of his time and unlike the rest of his designer house, this room actually felt like home.

"Finally, a room that looks lived in," Andrea commented.

"You didn't see this room when you were snooping around last night?"

"I didn't get this far."

She sat down on the brown leather couch, and he took a chair opposite from her, knowing that he couldn't allow himself to get too physically close to her or he'd lose what little control he had left. She'd already breached most of his walls and the rest of them were starting to crack.

"How are you feeling?" she asked. "Does your hand hurt?"

"It's fine. I threw a bad punch. Mick is going to be all over me about that."

She gave him a faint smile. "I'm glad you weren't hurt worse."

"I'm happy you weren't hurt at all. I never thought I was putting you in a dangerous situation when we went to get Tyler."

"It all happened really fast."

"So what do you want to ask me now?"

She stared back at him, uncertainty in her blue eyes, and that surprised him.

"Really? I've left you speechless?" he asked.

"I need to tell you something, Alex."

He didn't like the tone in her voice. "What's that?"

"When I was in your kitchen this morning, and you were getting ready to take Tyler to school, you got a text on you phone. It was on the counter, and it flashed right in front of me. I couldn't help but read it.

He stiffened, knowing exactly what she'd read.

"It was from your mother," Andrea continued. "I'm sure you remember what it said."

"I can't believe you looked at my phone."

"It wasn't intentional."

"It was just an opportunity."

She gave a guilty shrug.

"You went to meet her, didn't you?" A wave of anger ran through him. "You saw your chance, and you took it. How can I be surprised? I let you into my house. I put you in a position to do just what you did."

She gave him an apologetic look. "I'm sorry, Alex."

He got to his feet, too restless and furious to sit. "Don't bother to pretend that you have a conscience."

"I do have a conscience, which is why I didn't ask her anything about you."

"I don't believe you."

"It's the truth," she said, a pleading note in her voice as she stood up. "I was going to talk to her, Alex. I admit that. I wanted to ask her why everyone thinks she's dead and what happened to your father, and a dozen other things. But when I saw her face, and her eyes, so much like *your* eyes, I couldn't do it."

"You just walked away? You didn't say one word to her."

"I did introduce myself but that was it. She started to talk to me, and I told her I was a reporter, and I needed to hear the story from you, not from her. She didn't tell me anything, I swear."

Even if he could believe that, it didn't negate the fact that she'd gone behind his back to talk to his mother.

"Why did you let the world think she was dead, Alex? What happened to your father? How did you end up in foster care? And who is the pink bedroom for? Please talk to me."

He paced around the room, debating his options. The truth

was he had no options. All he could do was surrender to the inevitable. He sat back down, motioning Andrea to the couch. "You might as well sit. This will take a few minutes."

She perched on the edge of the couch.

He drew in a long, deep breath. "I haven't talked about any of this in probably a decade."

"Take your time."

"My mother, Rose, was born to older parents in a small town in Nebraska. She wanted to be a famous actress. When she was eighteen she moved to Hollywood, but it wasn't what she thought. Occasionally, she got to work as an extra on a TV show or in a movie," he continued, "but her main source of income came from her job as a cocktail waitress. She met my father in that bar. He was a dentist, not at all the kind of man she was used to hanging out with. He knocked her up about three months after they met. They were shocked by the unplanned pregnancy, but apparently in love, so they ran off to Vegas and got married." He paused. "She used to tell me it was the best three years of her life. But they broke up before my third birthday. My father had gone to a dental conference in Canada and had apparently fallen in love with another dentist he met there. My mother was heartbroken when he left us."

Alex cleared his throat, seeing the patient expression on Andrea's face as she waited for him to continue.

"My mother's dreams were shattered. She didn't have a husband, and her career was in the toilet. Oh, and there was that kid she had to take care of, too. To make herself feel better, she drank and got high. By the time I was six, I was taking care of her and trying to make sure she remembered to pick up food for us." He saw the gleam in Andrea's eyes. "Yeah, I guess my hoarding of food goes back to those early days."

"That's understandable."

"As my mother's problems worsened, she couldn't keep jobs. She drifted from man to man, letting anyone who would pay the bills move in for awhile."

"Oh, Alex," Andrea said softly. "I'm sorry."

"Don't interrupt." He held up a hand. "You wanted to know the story, and I'm only going to tell it once."

"Sorry. Go ahead."

"When I was ten, my mother met a musician. This guy was a cut above the others. He was talented, and he was in a successful band that was touring around the world. He wanted her to go with him, and she wanted to go, because she was in love. Unfortunately, she had me to worry about. She wanted to send me to Nebraska to live with my grandparents for a few months, but they were getting older, and my grandfather said they weren't up to taking me."

He could still remember when she'd shown him pictures of the farm in Nebraska. He'd wanted to go there. He'd thought it would be a lot better to live in a place with trees and land and horses to ride. But then his grandparents had said no, his mother had been furious, saying they never ever wanted to help her. He'd tried to make her feel better, but the only thing that could do that was a bottle of vodka.

Shaking his head, he forced his mind back to the story. "About a week later, she took me to a church and told me the priest was going to help her find a babysitter for me. She told me to wait there; she'd be back soon." His muscles tightened at the memory of that horrible day. The church had been big and dark and cold. He could still feel the hard pew under his ass and the terror of being alone, the certainty that he would never see his mother again.

"She didn't come back, did she?" Andrea asked, worry in her eyes.

"No, she never came back. The priest turned me over to Child Protective Services. They put me in foster care while they looked for my mother. They couldn't find her for months. She'd gotten on a plane and flown to Asia with her boyfriend's band. It was nine months before she was back in the states and by then she was in really bad shape. Her addictions had gotten worse. Her boyfriend was gone, and she was homeless. She came to see me, and she promised she'd go into rehab, and she did. I was hopeful she'd get better and she'd come back and get me. But she left rehab after two weeks and disappeared again. For the next several years I bounced around foster homes, and tried to survive while my mother periodically went in and out of rehab. At some point her parental rights were terminated, but it didn't matter to me. She was as good as dead to me."

"So when you spoke of her, you just killed her off," Andrea said.

"Her dying in a car accident was a much kinder version of the story," he said harshly.

"I agree. What about your father? Why didn't he come back and get you? And why couldn't my investigator find any trace of him?"

"He was killed in a car accident six months after he left us. He was living in Canada at the time, which is probably why your investigator couldn't trace him. If he'd never left us for that woman, maybe he'd be alive today. And that part of my car accident story was true."

"What about aunts, uncles, grandparents? Wasn't there anyone who could take you out of the system?"

"My grandparents came to see me once after my mother disappeared, but they said they couldn't take me in. I was better off in foster care. My grandmother gave me a St. Christopher medal and told me it would protect me. Some kid ripped it off my neck a few months later."

"This is a horrible story," Andrea murmured.

"You wanted to hear it," he reminded her. "As I got older, I got into trouble. I was angry at the world, and I hated the people I had to live with. When I was sixteen, I met Mick at the gym. He helped me redirect my anger, and he introduced me to a woman named Suzanne. She'd lost her daughter to a childhood cancer, and she had an empty room in her house. She also had a big heart. She took me in, and my life changed. It was the first time anyone had ever really cared about me. I called her my aunt, because it made life simpler. Unfortunately, she died less than two years later, and I was on my own again. The rest—you know." He blew out a breath, feeling a little relieved to have all his cards on the table—or almost all.

"I understand now why you didn't want to meet your mother," Andrea said slowly. "If I'd know what she'd done to you, I might have shoved her off the pier."

He appreciated the anger in Andrea's eyes and her desire to get him some justice. "I wouldn't have minded that."

"I have to say though, the woman I met earlier today looked very well-off though, not like an addict or a homeless person. She had a large diamond ring on her hand. Her circumstances obviously changed at some point."

"They did. Last year my mother showed up at my office one day and told me she'd changed her life. To say I was shocked to see her would be an understatement. It had been more than a decade since we'd been in the same room."

"I can't even imagine."

"My first thought was that she'd read about me and wanted money. I was going to kick her out, but she pleaded with me to listen to her. She said she'd met a man who had changed her life. She'd married him, and she'd been clean for eight years. She also had two little girls, my half-sisters, and she wanted them to meet me. She didn't want money; she wanted to reunite her family. She wanted me back in her life."

Andrea stared back at him. "What did you tell her?"

"I told her to get out. It was too late to make up for

anything. When she told me she wasn't going to leave until I heard her whole story, I walked out on her."

"And you haven't seen her since then?"

"No. I haven't seen her, but she wrote to me, called my office, left dozens of messages, each one telling me more about her daughters. She'd tell me about the Halloween parade at their school or the Christmas pageant, giving me dates and times in case I wanted to come. I never thought I would go, but one day I found myself standing outside an elementary school watching a bunch of kids parade down a sidewalk. I saw two little dark-haired girls run to my mother and give her a hug. There was a lot of love between them," he said, the reminder bringing another wave of pain. "It was strange to see her being a mother to another child, to two other children. I don't think she ever came to my school."

"She obviously changed after she got clean. Did you talk to your sisters?"

"No, I got in my car and drove away. But the calls from my mother kept coming. A week ago she started texting me on my cell phone. I didn't know how she got the number. I was going to change it, but I hadn't gotten around to it yet"

"Maybe subconsciously you didn't want to cut the last tie between you," Andrea suggested.

"I don't know why I wouldn't. You heard the story. She was a horrible mother. She threw me away, Andrea. Why would I want her back in my life?"

Andrea gave him a compassionate smile. "Because she's your mother." She gave him a speculative look. "The pink bedroom is for your sisters, isn't it?"

He nodded. "It was an impulsive decision. They've never met me, never been in this house, and I doubt they ever will."

"Why can't they come over? Why can't you meet them? They're your sisters, and they're not responsible for what your mother did."

"No, they're not responsible. They're beautiful, innocent little girls who adore their mother and their father. Zoe and Claire are the reason my past can't be made public. If I tell the world what my mother did, they'll eventually hear the story. They'll have to grow up wondering if their mother might abandon them." He paused. "And even if they're too young to understand it now, they could be impacted by what happens when my mother's husband finds out what kind of woman he married."

"Are you sure he doesn't know?"

"No, but I seriously doubt she would tell him everything. At any rate, I don't want to take that risk. I don't want Zoe and Claire to grow up without a father or with a mother suddenly being sent into another downward spiral when her husband takes off. I can't destroy their childhood. I can't put them through what I lived through. Can you understand that?" he asked forcefully. "It's not my mother I want to protect. It's not my reputation—I don't give a damn about that. This is about my sisters. They're children. It's up to me to protect them. I want them to have the happy childhood I didn't have. When they're older, they can know everything, but not now. Not from me. And most importantly, not from you."

She sucked in a quick breath. "Do you know what you're asking, Alex?"

"Yes." He met her gaze head-on. "I'm asking you not to tell the world about my past, about my mother. I know it will make your story better, and you have a career to build, but I'm asking you not to go there."

"I need to think," she said slowly.

It was not the answer he wanted to hear. "Do you really need time to think about whether or not it's worth protecting two innocent children?"

"That's not fair, Alex. You've given me three seconds to digest this information."

He got to his feet. "You should go then, and think—think hard. Then do what you need to do."

She stood up and pulled an envelope out of her bag. "I really don't want to give this to you now, but your mother asked me to make sure you received it, and I promised her I would do that. So here it is."

He couldn't bring himself to take the letter.

Andrea put it on the table, then walked out of the room.

He followed her to the front door, waiting for her to stop, to tell him that she would keep his secrets, that she would protect his sisters, that she would protect him... But she left without a word.

Chapter Fourteen

Andrea was still thinking about what she wanted to do with Alex's story when she walked into her office building just after eight on Friday morning. She was tired and in a bad mood, having once again slept very little the night before. Alex's story had gone around and around in her head. She could still hear the pain in his voice and see the hurt in his eyes when he spoke about being abandoned by his mother. He'd opened up to her, and he'd begged her to keep his secrets. A part of her really wanted to do that. The other part of her knew she still had to come up with a worthy cover story or her job would be on the line.

She needed to figure something out fast because her boss was standing by the receptionist's desk when she entered the lobby.

"How's it going with Donovan?" Roger asked, falling into step with her as she walked towards her cubicle. "I'm really hoping there's more to his story than just benevolent millionaire."

"That's a pretty good story on its own. You said it yourself when you gave me the assignment. Everyone likes a good success story, and Alexander Donovan is certainly that. Plus, he's a rich, attractive bachelor. You'll get the women readers with just that."

He gave her a speculative look. "What is wrong with you?"

"I don't know what you mean."

"You sound like you're going to give me the same story Alex has given every other news outlet in town. This is the cover, Andrea. We need something no one else has. You've been following the guy around all week. Surely, you've come up with more?"

She shrugged. "Not really, and I can't make something up, Roger."

"I'm not asking you to do that, but there's not a man alive who doesn't have a few embarrassments or skeletons in the closet. Keep looking. Are you seeing him this weekend?"

"No, it's my sister's bachelorette weekend. I'm leaving for Napa tonight. I'll follow up with Alex on Monday."

Roger didn't look happy at that piece of information. "I need a draft by next Wednesday."

"You'll have it."

As Roger left, she sat down at her desk with a sigh. She didn't have to keep looking for more dirt on Alex. She knew everything now, every little dirty secret. It was what to do with that information that she didn't know.

Alex had done an amazing job pulling himself out of the hole his mother had thrown him into when he was ten years old. All his success was a testament to his strong spirit, his determination to find a better life, his willingness to keep looking up and out instead of wallowing in the darkness.

He'd done it all on his own, and in many ways he was still on his own. She wondered if keeping the secret of his past was why he hadn't become seriously involved with anyone. Or maybe that reluctance went deeper than secrets. He'd loved his mother, and she'd rejected him, abandoned him, broken the most sacred trust of all, that between a mother and a child. It would be completely understandable if Alex had a problem with trust.

She'd broken his trust, too, she thought with a sorrowful sigh. By reading that text and going to see his mother, she'd betrayed him. He'd let her into his house. She'd used the advantage she'd gotten to get what she needed—a better story.

Roger would like her initiative, but she just felt bad. And she had no idea what to do next.

Alex had asked her to keep his secret, to protect his half-sisters and maybe to protect him, too, although he hadn't come right out and said that. He'd put it all on her, and there was a big part of her that wished she'd never learned the truth. But she had, and she had to deal with it. She had to make a decision that would affect a lot of people, including herself.

* * *

Friday afternoon, Alex walked past Fisherman's Wharf on his way to Pier 39. It was a sunny day and there were plenty of tourists enjoying the unusually warm weather. But he wasn't here to have fun. He was going to meet his mother. After reading her letter, he'd texted her back saying same place, same time. He hadn't wanted to invite her to his house or to his office. They would meet on neutral ground, and then maybe he could figure out how he wanted to proceed.

Sometimes the life he'd had with her seemed like a dream. At other times, he could vividly remember the one-bedroom apartment they'd shared and the years he'd spent sleeping on a beat-up couch with springs poking out of the cushions. Thinking back, he shouldn't have been that sad when she left him at the church, because life hadn't been that great with her. But she'd been his mother, the only family he had.

It shouldn't still hurt, he told himself. He was a grown man. He'd lived a lot of life since he'd been with her.

Still, as he walked down the pier toward the carousel, his

steps began to slow.

The fact that she'd chosen this place to meet wasn't lost on him. One of their favorite things to do in Los Angeles when he was a kid was to ride the merry-go-round at Griffith Park. She'd tell him to pick two of the fastest horses, and they'd ride around and around until they ran out of tickets. It was one of the only good memories he had of her.

He wished he didn't have that one. He wanted to hang on to the hate, to the anger. Those were far easier emotions to deal with.

He saw her before she saw him. Then she turned, and their eyes met.

An unexpected pain shot through his heart. No matter how much he hated her, she was still his mother, she was still the woman he'd prayed would come back to rescue him.

She had come back. Not to rescue him, but to make amends, to ask for forgiveness.

Why should he forgive her? Wasn't that just one more example of her putting herself before him?

What the hell was he doing here?

He stopped walking.

She must have sensed that he was about to flee, because she quickly came towards him, her gaze fixed on his face.

She stopped two feet away. "Alex," she murmured.

There were tears in her green eyes—eyes that were so like his own.

"Thank you for coming," she added.

"I don't really know why I did," he said, unable to look away from her. Her face looked good, far better than when he used to see her with pale, hollowed-out cheeks, pasty skin, and rotting teeth. Somewhere along the line, she'd fixed her teeth, colored her hair brown, put on some weight and invested in some good skin care products, because there was very little sign of the addict she'd once been. He'd bet a lot of money that the people who knew her now would be shocked to know how she'd once lived her life.

"Did you get my letter?" she asked. "I wasn't sure that woman I met would give it to you."

"She did."

"Did you read it?"

"Yes." Her letter had been filled with apologies. She was trying to take responsibility for all her bad choices. She wanted to be a better mother. She wanted to bring her family back together—her whole family.

"What did you think?"

"I honestly don't know what to think about you."

She shook a little under his hard gaze. "I know that you're still very angry, but I want you to meet your sisters, Alex. I want them to know you."

"Isn't that going to bring up a lot of questions for you? Does your husband know about your past?"

She let out a sigh. "Scott knows some of it. I've told him about my addiction problems."

"But he doesn't know the whole story?"

"He knows that I couldn't take care of you, but he doesn't know about the day I left you at the church."

"Why not?"

"I guess I was afraid that while he could accept my addictions, he wouldn't be able to accept the cruelty I showed you that day." She paused, giving him a pleading look. "I don't want to lose him, Alex. Not just because it would hurt me, but also because it would devastate the girls. And I've changed my life. I'm not the person who did those horrible things."

"You can't pretend you aren't that person," he said, shaking his head. "You can't act like it never happened."

"I didn't mean it that way. I just want you to understand that I've really changed. I'm not being controlled by drugs or alcohol any longer, and I'm trying to make a good life for my children and my husband."

"I don't really care what you do with your life," he said harshly.

She flinched, but her gaze didn't waver. "I get that. But I needed to say I was sorry and for you to hear me."

"That's what *you* needed. Did you ever think about what I needed?"

"I thought about it for a long time." She paused. "Leaving you at that church was the worst thing I've ever done in my life. I had nightmares about it for years. I kept seeing your sad face, and even though I didn't say good-bye, you knew I wasn't coming back."

She was right. He had known. He had known it from the second they left the apartment that that day was different.

"I told myself you'd be better off with another family, a good family," she added. "I was such a mess."

"Is that what you told yourself so you could sleep at night?"

"No. I never slept. I just passed out when my body couldn't take any more. I don't know how I lived through those years. I could have died so many times. But somehow I came out of it. Unfortunately, by the time that happened, you were all grown up. I thought about reaching out to you for a long time, but I always stopped myself. I couldn't imagine why you would want to see me. But after I got married and had the girls, I missed you even more. When I was mothering them, I was seeing you. That's why I finally came to see you last year. I know you thought I wanted money. That wasn't it at all. I wanted to see you, to tell you about the girls, to let you know that if there was any small part of you that wanted a family again, that we were there." She let out a breath. "Is there any small part of you that wants that?"

He thought about her question for a long moment. He wanted to know his sisters. He just needed to accept that they came with his mother.

Maybe it was time to let the past go. In reality, he probably wouldn't be the man he was today if she hadn't left him at that church. The fact that his life wasn't easy had pushed him to the level of success he had now.

Bottom line, he was tired of trying to avoid her and being angry with her. He'd always prided himself on being able to look forward, so why was he letting the past hold him back now?

"What do you say, Alex?" she pressed. "Will you at least think about it?"

"Aren't you afraid of what I'll tell my sisters or your husband about you?"

"I'm hoping I can trust you not to hurt them. You always protected people—from the time you were a little boy. You always stood up when anyone was getting picked on. You even tried to protect me. I remember all the times you came looking for me. You pulled me out of a bar one night, and you were only ten years old." Her eyes filled with pain. "I remember you holding my hair when I threw up. And then you told everything would be okay; you would take care of me. I was supposed to be taking care of you."

Her words hit him hard. She was the only one in the world who really knew his life, who'd lived those years with him.

"If I could change the past, I would, Alex. I'd be a better mother."

"Be a good mother now. Give those girls what you couldn't give me. If you want to make something up to me, do that."

"Will you meet your sisters?"

He hesitated. "I need a little time to think."

"I'll take that as a maybe. I'm glad we finally got a chance to talk." She paused. "That woman who came here yesterday—she said she was a reporter. Did you tell her our story?"

"I did."

Her face paled. "Do I need to prepare the girls?"

"I'm not sure yet." He paused. "I'm hoping Andrea will do the right thing."

"Do you really think you can trust a reporter? Or is she more to you than that?"

"I honestly don't know."

* * *

Later that night, Alex worked off the stress of seeing his mother again at Mick's gym. After thirty minutes pounding a punching bag with his one good hand, he was starting to feel slightly more in control of his life. He took a break, pulled off his glove and grabbed a bottle of water out of the refrigerator.

As he was taking a long swig, Mick walked over to him.

"Who were you beating the crap out of?" Mick asked.

"I'm not sure. A lot of people have been pissing me off lately."

"Including yourself?"

Alex frowned, wondering how Mick was always able to get to the heart of the matter. "Yeah, I was in the mix," he admitted, taking another drink of water.

"Who else? Andrea?"

Andrea's pretty face and sparkling blue eyes flashed through his head, but along with her image came anger and the sense of betrayal. She'd violated his privacy. She'd gone to meet his mother. Maybe in the end her conscience had stopped her from going forward, but he couldn't forget just how far she had gone.

"I think I hit the jackpot," Mick said, tossing him a towel.

Alex wiped the sweat off of his face. "She went to meet

my mother."

Mick blew out a whistle of amazement. "No shit? How did that happen?"

"She saw a text from my mom on my phone. I told you my mother somehow got my cell number."

"What did your mother tell Andrea?" Mick asked, his expression more somber now.

"Apparently nothing. Andrea had second thoughts about what she was doing and quickly bailed out of the meeting."

Mick smiled. "That's good to hear."

"Is it? She's an ambitious reporter. Maybe she balked at pumping my mother for information, but who knows what she'll do next? I can't trust her, Mick."

"But you want to, because you like her."

"Yeah, I like her, but I don't like that side of her."

"It sounds to me like she did the right thing in the end."

"I can't forget what she did in the beginning. She betrayed me."

"Did she, Alex? You knew all along she was a reporter. She wasn't working undercover. You didn't need to let her into your house, give her access to your phone."

"You're right. I knew all along what she was about. I just didn't want to see it, because I wanted her to be different."

"Why would you want her to be different than who she is? She's smart, beautiful, strong, courageous, and I think she has a good heart. She's a fighter, Alex. And so are you. Or at least you used to be. Why don't you fight for her?"

"Before or after she rips my life apart with her magazine article?" he challenged.

"I thought you said your mother didn't tell her anything."

"She didn't, but I did. I told her the whole sordid story, because I figured she was going to eventually get to the truth on her own."

Mick nodded approvingly. "Good. You needed to let it all

out. It's been festering inside of you for too long."

"It's not good," he protested. "I know you think I've stayed quiet to protect my mother or maybe even myself. But it's really about the girls now, about my sisters."

"I believe you, Alex. You've always watched out for the innocent. But I think Andrea is going to find a way to write a good article and do right by you at the same time."

"I don't see how she possibly could."

"Don't underestimate her, Alex."

Was he underestimating her? "I guess I'll have to see what happens."

"I guess you will."

Chapter Fifteen

It had been sixteen days since she'd seen Alex, Andrea realized, as she zipped herself into her bridesmaid's dress. She'd kept herself busy with work and wedding events, managing to get her article written as well as participate in her sister's bachelorette weekend, bridal shower, rehearsal dinner and now the wedding. But all the while Alex had been on her mind. She couldn't believe how much she missed him. It was a deep ache that started in her heart and spread to every nerve ending in her body.

She'd thought of calling him so many times, but she'd always stopped herself. She'd wanted him to reach out to her first. And since her article had come out the day before, she'd been checking her phone even more frequently. But he hadn't called. Maybe what she'd written hadn't made a difference.

She sighed as she looked in the mirror and told herself she was a fool for thinking he'd get in touch. Alex was a man who needed a woman in his life he could trust, and that wasn't her.

"Why are you looking so glum?" Liz asked, coming up behind her.

She turned to her friend and fellow bridesmaid and forced a smile on herself. "I was just lost in thought."

"Thinking about Alex?"

She frowned, wishing she hadn't shared her feelings for

Alex at the bachelorette party, but after a couple of glasses of champagne, she'd found herself confessing everything to her friends—not the part about Alex's past, but the part where she'd let herself fall in love with the man she was supposed to be profiling. She hadn't told them about her betrayal either; she'd just hinted that she'd been a little too ambitious and thought she'd hurt him. They'd all been intensely curious, but good friends that they were, they hadn't asked too many questions. They'd just tried to cheer her up and make her feel better.

"I did let myself go there," she admitted. "But I'm done. Today is about Laurel. Is she finished with her pictures yet?" Her mom and sister had been taking some photographs in the garden outside the church for the last half hour.

"Yes, she's her way here," Liz replied.

"Great." Andrea turned back to face the mirror. "We don't look too bad."

"No, we don't," Liz agreed. "I'll never wear this dress again, but at least it's not hideous, just really frilly."

The lacey mint green dress was not Andrea's taste either, but it fit perfectly with Laurel's vision. She smiled at Liz. "The first dress of many."

Liz smiled back at her. "Well, no one else seems to be even close to getting engaged, so hopefully bridesmaids dresses will improve before the next wedding."

Andrea laughed. "I seriously doubt it. By the way, how is your dad?"

"He's a little better, but he has officially retired from the company, which is going to make my life more challenging. I'm going to have to make myself extremely valuable to his partners or they'll find a way to kick me out."

"What are you going to do?"

"I'm in the running for a big new account worth millions of dollars. If I can bring it in, the partners won't have any choice but to keep me, and then I can keep my dad's legacy alive."

"I wish you luck."

"Thanks. I think I'm going to need it."

As Liz finished speaking, the door to the church dressing room opened, and the bride and the rest of the bridal party poured into the room. Jessica had arrived the night before from San Diego with her six-year-old son, Braden. Andrea adored Braden. He and Jessica had slept on her pull-out couch the night before, and she'd had some time to catch up with Jess whose divorce had left her reeling but determined to make a better life for herself.

"Hi Andrea," Braden said. "I'm going to carry the rings."

She smiled at the proud look in his eyes. "I know. I can't wait to see you walk down the aisle." Braden was completely adorable in his black suit and dark green tie.

"I just hope he doesn't drop the pillow," Jessica said.

"He'll do just fine."

"Everyone looks so beautiful," Jessica added, wistfulness in her voice. "I really wish I'd done my wedding right the first time."

"You'll have another chance," Andrea assured her. "And we'll all be there for you the next time."

"Well, it won't be any time soon."

"We have time for one toast," Kate interrupted as she and Liz quickly handed out glasses of champagne. "Andrea, do you want to do the honors?"

"Yes." She looked at her sister, her gorgeous, glowing twin sister, and her heart swelled with love and pride. "To Laurel, an amazing daughter, a wonderful sister, and a caring and loyal friend. May today be the start of a future of happiness and love. You deserve it all. And I wouldn't mind a niece or nephew, either."

Laurel laughed. "One step at a time."

"To Laurel," Liz put in.

"And to all of you," Laurel said. "I love every single one of you and you better not cut me out of the fun, just because I'm going to be a boring, married woman now."

"Never," Andrea said as they clinked their glasses together.

* * *

The candlelit wedding ceremony was romantic and perfect in every way. Laurel and her groom looked at each other through the eyes of adoring love, and Andrea felt herself getting misty-eyed more than once, especially during the exchange of vows.

She'd never really thought much about marriage. When her mom and sister talked about it, she usually tuned them out. She'd always had her eye on her career, on getting to the next rung of the ladder, making a name for herself, but now she couldn't help wondering if her goals weren't a little narrow.

Why couldn't she have it all—a job and a relationship? It would be more difficult, but she was up to the challenge. She just had to find the right man.

Actually, she'd already found the right man, but she'd messed everything up.

She forced herself not to think about Alex. She had to focus on her sisters, her friends and her family. Alex was a worry for another day.

After the ceremony, there was almost an hour of pictures. Then they moved on to dinner, toasts and eventually cake-cutting. As waiters passed out slices of cake, Laurel walked over to Andrea and gave her a hug.

"What was that for?" Andrea asked.

"Everything," Laurel said. "You've been a great maid of honor."

She laughed. "You have a short memory, but thanks. Are you happy, Laurel? Was today everything you imagined?"

"It was better than my best dream. And I don't think I've ever felt happier. I can't wait to get our marriage started."

"I think you already have, and I'm glad you found a man who loves you so much."

"Your turn will come, Andrea."

She shrugged. "I'm not holding my breath."

"You might meet someone tonight—someone tall, dark and handsome," Laurel said with a sparkle in her eyes.

"If that man is actually here, then he's probably already surrounded by your six other single bridesmaids," she said, taking a sip of champagne.

"Actually, I think he's looking for you." Laurel tipped her head to the right.

Andrea turned around and saw Alex standing by the bar. He was dressed in a black suit with a dark red tie, and he was just as tall, dark and handsome as Laurel had said. Butterflies danced through her stomach as she met his gaze.

"Isn't that your man of the year?" Laurel asked.

"He's not *my* man," she muttered, her gaze on Alex as he slowly made his way toward them.

"Are you sure about that? I know you never take my advice, Andrea, but give him a chance. You could do worse than a sexy millionaire."

Laurel slipped away when Alex reached her. As his beautiful green gaze met hers, her heart began to beat in triple time.

"I can't believe you're here," she said in amazement. "Why are you here?"

"I wanted to see you."

Her breath caught in her throat at the simple, direct statement. "Really? Because the last two weeks…"

"I know," he interrupted. "The last two weeks have been

the worst weeks of my life."

"Were you that worried about the article?"

"I was more worried that I was never going to see you again, that I'd screwed everything up."

"I'm the one who did that."

"Can we go somewhere and talk for a moment?"

"Sure," she said, leading him through the ballroom to the patio.

It was a cool night, and Alex immediately slipped off his coat and wrapped it around her shoulders, just as he'd done the night he'd taken her to the airport to watch the planes take off.

"Are you warm enough?" he asked.

It was funny that Alex would have such good manners growing up the way he did. Somewhere along the way, he'd learned how to be thoughtful, or maybe it was just his nature.

"I'm fine." She could feel Alex's heat still clinging to his coat. It was almost as if his arms were around her. "Did you read the article?" She hated to bring it up, but they couldn't ignore the elephant in the room.

He nodded. "I did. It wasn't exciting or groundbreaking, but it was well written. How did your boss like it?"

"He had much the same impression. Competent was the word he used to describe it."

"Are you in trouble?"

"Let's just say they won't be handing me any plum assignments for a while."

He gazed into her eyes. "Why didn't you tell the whole story, Andrea?"

She let out a sigh. "Because it belongs to you, Alex. You're the only one who should tell it. I personally think the way you rose from such despairing circumstances would inspire a lot of people, but I understand that it's complicated and that you want to protect your sisters." She paused. "Maybe you want to protect your mother, too."

He frowned. "I wouldn't go that far."

"Did you read her letter?"

"Yes. Did you?"

"No." She shouldn't have been surprised by the question, but it disappointed her. It showed her that Alex still didn't trust her. "I don't open private mail."

"Not even for the scoop of a lifetime?"

"It wasn't going to be that. It was a letter from a mother to a son."

"But without reading the letter, how would you know that?" he challenged.

"When I spoke to your mother, I saw the pain and regret in her eyes. I knew that letter was personal." She paused. "I think we should get something straight. I'm a good reporter, and if I'm after a news story that I think will hugely impact someone's life or expose corruption or greed or fraud or anything like that, I will go all out. I would probably read a letter or intercept a text or do whatever I had to do to get to the truth. But it would only be for the greater good. And maybe you think that makes me unethical or untrustworthy, I don't know, but I can't lie and I can't apologize for what I do. Reporters dig. That's my job, and I do it the best way I know how."

"Are you done?"

"Yes," she said.

"Then can I talk now?"

"I've never tried to stop you from talking," she reminded him. "So go for it."

"I went to see my mother the day after you gave me the letter. We had a brief conversation then and another one last night. She was relieved that you didn't include her in your story or any mention of my sisters. She told me that you must really care about me if you would keep my secrets." He paused. "Do you care about me, Andrea?"

She sucked in a breath, wanting to protect herself from rejection but also wanting him to know how she felt. "Yes."

His smile broadened and his eyes sparkled with what looked like relief. "I'm glad to hear that, because I feel the same way. I know I put you in a difficult position. I should never have agreed to the interview. I just didn't expect the story to be anything deeper than I'd done in the past. You were doing your job, and I probably hurt your career by asking you to keep my secrets. If there is anything I can do to help you out there, I will. I also heard what you just said, and I have absolutely no doubts about your level of integrity. None."

"I'm glad to hear that."

"He took her hands in his. "I want to start over, Andrea. No interview, no secrets, no lies between us. What do you think?"

She thought it was the most wonderful idea she'd ever heard. "I'm in," she said with a smile.

He smiled back at her. "Good. I'm not very good at relationships, but I want you to know that I'm going to try really hard not to hurt you."

"Same here. You can trust me Alex. I know that may be hard for you to believe—"

"It's not," he said, cutting her off. "If I didn't believe I could trust you, I wouldn't be here." He took a breath, then added, "I've always resisted love, because it's usually followed by pain. Every time I love someone or something, they disappear. It's been easier not to care. But I don't want easy if it means you're not in my life."

She was touched by his words. "I'm not going anywhere," she said, putting her hands on his face. "I'm in love with you, Alex."

"I'm in love with you, too," he said, a husky note in his voice. His lips touched hers with passion, purpose and promise.

Then her sister's voice rang out, and they broke apart.

Laurel walked over to join them. "Sorry to interrupt," she said with a curious gleam in her eyes as she turned her gaze to Alex. "I don't think we've met."

"Alex Donovan. I apologize for the wedding crash, but I couldn't wait another minute to talk to your sister."

"It's very nice to meet you. So what's going on out here? Are you two together now..."

"We are," Andrea said as Alex put his arm around her shoulders.

"This is so exciting," Laurel said with delight in her eyes. "Come inside, both of you. Let's tell everyone."

"No way, this is your day," Andrea protested.

"You're my sister. I can't think of anything better than for you to fall in love on my wedding day. It's so romantic. And I am definitely throwing the wedding bouquet in your direction, so come on."

"Okay, okay," she said, giving in. "We'll be inside in a second."

As Laurel returned to the party, Andrea glanced back at Alex. "You do know my sister is going to start planning our wedding before the night is over."

"Really? That soon?"

"But that's her and my mother, not me," she said, wanting him to understand that she wasn't going to rush him into anything. "I just want to be with you. Whatever comes down the road we'll figure out together."

"I like the sound of that."

"But that won't stop the flood of questions you'll get as soon as we step into the ballroom together, so if you want to make a hasty exit—"

"I don't. After getting interviewed by you, I think I can handle any questions," he said dryly. "And it's not like I didn't put you in uncomfortable situations."

"That's right, you did. The awful boat ride was way worse than this," she agreed.

They laughed together at the memory.

"Ready to go inside and watch me catch the bouquet?" she asked.

"I have a better idea. Catch me instead." He put his arms around her, gave her a long, loving look and started a kiss that would last forever.

Epilogue

Liz Palmer watched Andrea enter the ballroom with the very attractive Alex Donovan at her side. Andrea's cheeks were bright red, her blue eyes sparkling as she pulled her hand out of Alex's grip and walked to the center of the dancer floor where the single women were getting ready for the bouquet toss.

"Where have you been?" Liz asked.

"Kissing Alex," Andrea said with a mischievous grin.

Liz laughed. "At least you're honest. Did you know he was coming? You didn't say anything earlier."

"I had no idea. He surprised me—in a lot of ways."

"Good ways?"

"Very good."

"Andrea?" Kate came forward with a question in her eyes. "Laurel said you have news and that I might have another wedding to plan soon. It's Alex, isn't it? I knew you two were going to fall in love. Didn't I say that the first time you went to meet him?"

"You did," Andrea said with a laugh. "But no wedding plans yet. Alex and I are just beginning."

"But you already love him," Liz said, feeling incredibly moved by the joyful glow in Andrea's eyes. She hadn't seen her friend this happy ever.

"I do," Andrea confessed. "I know it's fast, but I feel so sure that he's the one." She gave a helpless shrug. "I never really believed there was one perfect person for me, but now I know there is. Alex isn't perfect, and neither am I, but together we seem to make each other better."

"That's so beautiful," Kate said, giving Andrea a hug. "You're going to make me cry."

Liz felt moisture gathering in her own eyes, and she had never thought of herself as an emotional person. Andrea had never been all that sentimental either. In fact, up until about two minutes ago, she'd always considered Andrea to be her cynical counterpart when it came to love and romance. They had both been more focused on work and career than men and romance.

"No crying, this is a happy day," Andrea said, but her eyes were suspiciously wet.

Laurel stepped up to the microphone, drawing their attention to the bandstand. "Are you ready, ladies?" she asked.

The crowd of twenty or so single women cheered in response.

"Let's see who's going to be the next bride."

"I'm standing next to you, Andrea," Kate said. "I know who Laurel is going to be aiming for."

Liz moved off to the side as Julie and Maggie also closed in on Andrea, obviously sensing where the toss was headed. She wasn't interested in catching the bouquet. She had more important things to worry about than falling in love. She wouldn't even be out here if it wasn't required as part of her bridesmaid duties.

A drum roll began, and Laurel turned her back to the crowd. One, two, three—the bouquet of gorgeous white roses went flying through the air. A dozen women leapt for it, but Laurel's throw was remarkably strong and sailed over the crowd.

Liz was shocked when the bouquet literally hit her in the chest. She was three feet away from everyone else. She couldn't help but wrap her arms around the beautiful stems.

"Liz," Laurel squealed with delight as she rushed across the dance floor.

"You know what this means," Kate said with a gleam in her eyes.

"No," she said. "This is for you, Andrea." She tried to hand the bouquet to Andrea, who had obviously been Laurel's intended recipient.

"No way," Andrea said with a shake of her head. "You caught it. It's yours."

"You're going to be the next bride," Laurel said with a smile.

"I don't even have a boyfriend," she replied in bemusement.

"That could change at any second," Andrea said. "Look what happened to me."

"Let's get one more photo with all the bridesmaids," Kate said, gathering them together.

They stood in a half circle, their arms around each other, as the photographer took their picture. And right in the front was Liz and the wedding bouquet she'd never expected to catch.

It didn't mean anything, did it?

The End

* * * * *

Coming November 20, 2014

Steal My Heart
Bachelors & Bridesmaids (#2)

Was there no escaping her high school nemesis, Michael Stafford? Liz Palmer had had her first run-in with the football hero when he'd tried to kiss her in high school, and she'd broken his nose. Now ten years later Michael is back in her life, vying for the same business account, and she is determined to win.

Liz's career is her life, but something has been missing all these years, and in her heart she knows it's Michael. With her friends falling in love, and yet another stint as a bridesmaid in her future, Liz wonders if there's a way to mix business and love...

Dear Reader,

I hope you enjoyed reading Alex and Andrea's love story in KISS ME FOREVER, the first book in the Bachelors and Bridesmaids series about seven college friends who start out as bridesmaids and end up as brides!

The next book in the series, STEAL MY HEART, will be out November 20, 2014 with the third book, ALL YOUR LOVING, coming December 15, 2014.

I'm also writing a connected family series: The Callaways. Every book features love, romance, suspense and adventure. If you haven't met this intriguing family, check out the first book, ON A NIGHT LIKE THIS. The first seven books are currently available with book #8 SOMEWHERE ONLY WE KNOW coming out in January 2015.

Happy reading!

Barbara

Book List

About The Author

Barbara Freethy is a #1 New York Times Bestselling Author of 41 novels ranging from contemporary romance to romantic suspense and women's fiction. Traditionally published for many years, Barbara opened her own publishing company in 2011 and has since sold over 4.8 million ebooks! Nineteen of her titles have appeared on the New York Times and USA Today Bestseller Lists.

Known for her emotional and compelling stories of love, family, mystery and romance, Barbara enjoys writing about ordinary people caught up in extraordinary adventures. She is currently writing a connected family series, The Callaways, which includes: ON A NIGHT LIKE THIS (#1), SO THIS IS LOVE (#2), FALLING FOR A STRANGER (#3) BETWEEN NOW AND FOREVER (#4), ALL A HEART NEEDS (#5), THAT SUMMER NIGHT (#6) and WHEN SHADOWS FALL (#7). If you love series with romance, suspense and a little adventure, you'll love the Callaways.

Barbara also recently released the WISH SERIES, a series of books connected by the theme of wishes including: A SECRET WISH (#1), JUST A WISH AWAY (#2) and WHEN WISHES COLLIDE (#3).

Other popular standalone titles include: DON'T SAY A WORD, SILENT RUN, SILENT FALL, and RYAN'S RETURN.

Barbara's books have won numerous awards - she is a six-time finalist for the RITA for best contemporary romance from Romance Writers of America and a two-time winner for DANIEL'S GIFT and THE WAY BACK HOME.

Barbara has lived all over the state of California and currently resides in Northern California where she draws much of her inspiration from the beautiful bay area.

For a complete listing of books, as well as excerpts and contests, and to connect with Barbara:

Visit Barbara's Website:
www.barbarafreethy.com
Join Barbara on Facebook:
www.facebook.com/barbarafreethybooks
Follow Barbara on Twitter:
www.twitter.com/barbarafreethy

Made in the USA
Monee, IL
29 December 2021

87468430R00108